The Witch's Kiss

by

Tricia Schneider

The Merriweather Witches Series

The Witch's Kiss

Cover Art by *Debbie Taylor*

The Wild Rose Press, Inc.
PO Box 708
Adams Basin, NY 14410-0708
Visit us at www.thewildrosepress.com

Publishing History
First Black Rose Edition, 2015
Print ISBN 978-1-62830-750-4
Digital ISBN 978-1-62830-751-1

The Merriweather Witches Series
Published in the United States of America

"Do you ever wonder why I never
propositioned you?" Sage asked, the anger in his soul making him lash out. "I've been with many women. They call me the Merriweather Rake, did you know?" He laughed at the absurd moniker the ton had dubbed him. "Yet you are the only one I've never seduced."

She flinched.

He thought the pain spreading across her face would make him feel just in his cause. He needed to push her away. From the look on her face, he succeeded. Instead of the satisfaction he thought it might bring, he felt only pain.

Pain from her sadness, her suffering.

"You are a good man, Sage," she said with a slight tremor in her voice, the only sign she was affected by his cruel words. "Do not fool yourself."

She stood and walked away.

The lavender scent faded. Sage rubbed a hand over his eyes, trying to block the image of her sadness from his mind.

Had he done the right thing?

This curse confined Marianne to a select few. Essentially, she was forced to speak with him, spend time with him, even just for the pure sake of her sanity. What choice did she have when no one else could hear or see her?

Marianne was not to blame for the fact that Sage's feelings regarding her were changing, that when he looked at her he saw not a child with gangly limbs, but a woman full-grown. One who had become a close friend. And that he desired their friendship to grow into something much more…intimate.

Praise for Tricia Schneider

"I enjoyed *[THE WITCH AND THE WOLF]* so much that I was sad to see it come to an end. I look forward to seeing what else this author has to offer as this is one story I know I will read over and over again."

~Theresa Joseph, The Romance Studio
~*~

"*THE WITCH AND THE WOLF* grabs you in the beginning and holds you until the end."

~Stacey Krug, Siren Book Reviews
~*~

"Tricia Schneider has earned a new fan in this reviewer! Her writing flowed with poetic mastery, keeping me glued to the pages from the beginning until 'the end'. She created an atmosphere ripe with desire; from a look, to an innocent touch, to the grand finale, the romance divine."

~LynnMarie, Happily Ever After Reviews
~*~

"With its well-written storyline, and delightfully gothic mood throughout, [*THE WITCH AND THE VAMPIRE*] is an absolutely pleasurable reading experience."

~Laurie, Coffee Time Romance & More
~*~

"Tricia Schneider's writing makes you feel like you are right there living the story."

~Stacey Krug, Siren Book Reviews
~*~

"I couldn't flip the pages fast enough wondering how in the world would they triumph and get their happily ever after."

~Xeranthemum, Long and Short Reviews

Dedication

To my grandparents for all their love and support.
They encouraged me to follow my dreams
and never give up.
Thank you!

Chapter One

The dancing couples spun in colorful clouds of satins and silks. Sage Merriweather wandered the sidelines, his lengthy stature making it easy to search above the heads of the men and women occupying the crowded room.

"Ah, Sage, there you are! I've been searching for you."

He turned at the sound of his name. Marianne Grey walked toward him, swaying to the music as she deftly avoided contact with the near crush of guests that filled Winfield Park. Once she reached his side, she spun before him, holding her arms out in invitation.

"Won't you dance with me, Mr. Merriweather?" A twinkle of merriment lit her blue eyes. "It's been *an age* since anyone asked me to dance. And I do so love a waltz."

"Of course, my dear." Sage spoke through smiling teeth, his lips barely moving. "I can't imagine why anyone might care to call Bedlam when they see me waltzing with thin air."

Marianne sighed dramatically. "I'm not simply air. I'm a ghost. A spirit. A phantom. However, I *do* exist."

"True," he said. "And invisible to all but me."

"And my sister."

"Yes. Your sister who has sent her husband to introduce me to someone of importance. Someone who might have information to save you from this bodiless existence. So if you please, I have work to do. Why do you not watch the dancers perform? It's quite lovely and will keep you entertained while I attend to business."

Marianne's shoulders sank. "I cannot bear it any longer."

"You were happy as a lark moments ago."

"Yes, until you denied me a dance. I've never before been set down. Even without a body I find the insult unbearable."

Sage had the audacity to grin, which annoyed Marianne all the more. She bristled with wrath, lifting his sagging spirits at the sight. Of late, she had become more docile and glum, not at all like the feisty Marianne he had known for most of his twenty-eight years. Being neighbors in the small village of Meryton had thrown their families often together, enough so they became more than simply friends. They had become family. It became official after his brother and her sister wed four months ago.

"Are you not pleased to hear we might be at the end of our search for someone with knowledge to assist you?"

"Yes, of course," Marianne said. "But if I cannot dance, then what shall I do while I wait for you? Believe it if you will, but being a ghost is not all excitement. In fact, it's dreadfully dull."

"Then come with me," he suggested, still keeping his lips as stiff as possible when a couple nearby darted curious glances in his direction. He experienced difficulty at times when talking with Marianne in public. People took note when he spoke to no one.

"You may give your opinion of the man's character after we leave Winfield and return home."

Marianne nodded. He marveled again at the lifelike resemblance. If he reached out to touch her, instead of feeling flesh and bone, he'd sense nothing more than frigid air. Yet she stood, looking as real and alive as he, just as solid as anyone currently on this ballroom floor. It was remarkable to know that while her spirit stood in this room speaking, her body remained in one of the upstairs rooms in Merriweather Manor.

"Is that Basil?" Marianne tilted her head in the direction of the open doors leading to the gardens.

"Yes."

Together they pardoned their way through the dancers and wallflowers. At least Sage did so while Marianne did her best to avoid contact with anyone until they reached the edge of the mass of guests. Some rather sensitive people spoke of the cool air surrounding them.

Basil stood by the French doors, waiting until Sage approached.

"Come with me," he said, without any word of greeting.

Sage spared a glance at Marianne who shrugged. They both proceeded to follow as he led them onto the patio and down the steps leading to the giant fountain in the center of the garden. The sculpture boasted a trio of mermaids, entwined in an ethereal and slightly erotic dance, their faces stretching upward and mouths open in song. Rather than notes, a stream of water gurgled from their mouths. It was a peculiar piece of art, one which Sage hoped he'd never have the misfortune of seeing again.

Basil strode passed the hideous fountain until he came to the hedge outlining the massive labyrinth where couples wandered, all with smiles of anticipation. Sage took note that most who wandered out busily adjusted their clothes.

"In here," Basil said, stopping to face them. "I enlisted the help of someone I met while traveling the wilds of India. I've spoken to her, and she's agreed to meet you."

"India doesn't seem very wild," Marianne mumbled as she stepped beside Sage. "Not compared to that fountain, at least."

Sage suppressed a smirk before turning back to his brother.

"Her?"

"Her name is Desmonda Green," Basil said. "She will try to help. Marianne…" His gaze darted to either side of Sage. Seeing nothing, he inquired, "Is she here?"

Sage nodded to his left.

"This woman knows people who might have access to spells and other scientific knowledge. Alchemists and the like. She might offer some insight we haven't explored as of yet."

"What we need is a necromancer."

"We *had* a necromancer," Basil said, sharply. "It does not bode well for us to continue down that path. Marianne is not dead. She's merely…sleeping. In a deep, death-like sleep."

Sage grunted. They had searched every spell book and grimoire in Merriweather Manor and their London house in Mayfair. Sage's father had been a historian with a penchant for recording details of magic folk cultures and practices. Before his death, Philip Merriweather had taken it upon himself to record the known spells practiced by family, friends and other relations. He had collected such an extensive library the books needed to be hidden for fear they might be used as tools to those with darker intentions, such as Drake when he attempted to steal them last winter.

"What does she look like? This woman."

"Red hair," Basil answered. "Like fire. You won't mistake her."

"Very well." Sage attempted to ignore the chill suddenly creeping along his back. He took a step toward the entrance of the maze. Basil remained fixed in place. "Are you not coming?"

"No. I'm eager to return to the manor."

And to Julia...

His brother's unspoken words rang loud. Sage nodded, glad Basil had found the love of his life. While they traveled the English countryside searching for clues to aid their quest, Julia remained at Merriweather Manor swollen with Basil's child. It would not be long before another Merriweather entered this world, and he knew his brother itched to be back before the miraculous event occurred.

"Give Julia and Aunt Petunia my love."

"I will." Basil grasped his arm, slapping his back in a brotherly embrace. "Send word as soon as you can. Good luck."

Sage nodded. His brother walked back up the steps to disappear into the crowded house. Sage felt a momentary desire to follow. It would be so easy to give up this foolhardy quest. They had searched for months with no hope of a spell to help Marianne. She seemed doomed to remain a ghost forever. As for Sage, his difficulties were insurmountable. Nothing he did, not a spell or a plan of action, changed the darkness he had fallen into as of late. It became apparent that the demon's curse affected his very skin and bones. He had little hopes of ever escaping that bond. And his dreams of late had grown worse…

"Shall we?" Marianne's voice snapped him out of his dark reverie.

"Of course," he said, then reluctantly took the necessary steps toward the entrance.

"Would you like me to go first?" Marianne asked, no doubt aware of his hesitation. "I can alert you to any danger. After all, no one can harm what they cannot see."

"Do you sense danger?"

Marianne paused, considering. "Not danger. More like a threat."

That she possessed any of her witch talents marveled him, but now was not the time to dwell upon it. He sensed the same. The tiny hairs on the back of his neck lifted like a cool breeze had blown passed. Basil would never knowingly send him into danger, so he had nothing to fear. That did not mean he wouldn't take every precaution to keep Marianne's spirit safe.

To send a woman, even as a ghost, into the unknown to preserve his own safety simply would not do.

"No need, my dear. I'm certain our trepidation stems from mere excitement at the prospect of finally finding a new avenue for our search."

"Perhaps you are correct," Marianne conceded.

Sage nearly reached to take her hand. She needed

comfort. Her eyes were wide and her breath quickened, but he could not do anything as human as take her hand to squeeze her fingers in reassurance. She was a ghost. Humans, even witches, were unable to touch ghosts.

"Come along," he said instead and proceeded to walk into the maze. The walls of the trimmed hedge towered over him, a substantial distance considering his height. Lamps lit at incremental distances illuminated the path in the darkening twilight, giving the maze a gothic aura like something he might read in a novel. The murmurs and whispers of the guests reached his ears, but with no sight of people at present, the voices echoed like bodiless apparitions. To anyone else, the belief that monsters may exist might creep into their imagination sending a shiver of fear along their spines. Sage, who knew for a fact that monsters did indeed exist, took the precaution of walking warily along the path. He was well aware that evil lurked in dark corners, but that knowledge would not stop him in his search. He had faced evil and survived.

After several misguided attempts at traveling the maze, Sage began to lose his sense of direction. He had taken several turns, of which he lost count, and passed a few couples in as much confusion as he. Some guests had given up solving the puzzle of the labyrinth and decided to partake activities of the more sensual nature. They found hidden alcoves along the way and ensconced themselves there, hoping no one noticed the fornication taking place.

Again, he wished to touch Marianne so he might cover her innocent eyes from such carnal play. Although she was of marriageable age and had been introduced to society shortly before Drake cursed her, he was aware of her youth and innocence, something many a rake and scoundrel preyed upon during a night such as this.

A guilty flush crept along his neck as he realized less than a year ago he himself might have tempted her into a similar alcove for a night of seduction. Of course, this was Marianne, his neighbor and friend. He'd known her since she was in nappies. He could never have feelings of such a nature for her. He regarded her as a sister. And even as a rake, Sage always played the safer game of seducing widows or women unhappily wed to distant husbands. He was quite aware of marriage traps and stepped carefully to avoid them.

"There," Marianne whispered.

He turned in the direction she indicated. A woman dressed in a long silk gown of greenish hue akin to the color of an emerald stood alone. The vibrant red hair wrapped and braided in intricate design upon her head like curling flame in the dim light. The contrast between hair and gown was striking. He took in the beauty of her classical features as she stared boldly at him with one arched brow.

"Mr. Merriweather, I presume," she said, her voice husky with intrigue.

"I am," he answered, stopping a few paces in front of her. "I'm told you possess information I desire."

She smiled, sliding her hand lower on her hips. "I have many things you may desire."

Marianne made a distressed choking sound.

Sage didn't know whether to grin or be embarrassed. Although she was a grown woman, he still thought of Marianne as a child. He should protect her from women such as this, who might lead her into the temptation of baser natures, assisting her down a path best left untraveled for women of Marianne's status.

Then again, Marianne knew Sage to be a rake and a rogue, his habits of seducing women well known. She often made comments on his conquests, although he never acknowledged if she'd guessed rightly or not. He may behave as a rake, but he was still a gentleman.

"She cannot truly be serious," Marianne said, the disgust evident in the scorn dripping from her words.

"I believe she is." He did not bother to hide his obvious one-sided conversation. According to Basil, this woman was aware of Marianne's predicament.

The woman's chin tilted. Her gaze darted to Sage's left. "Your friend is here?"

Sage nodded and sighed for dramatic effect to irritate Marianne. "She rarely leaves my side."

"How unfortunate."

Marianne made another choking sound of disgust which only made Sage smile with amusement.

"May I present Miss Marianne Grey," Sage introduced with a wave toward Marianne. It seemed rather comical that the woman nodded toward what she could only see as space beside him.

"My name is Desmonda Green," the woman replied. "I was contacted a fortnight ago by your brother who requested I meet with you. Since I am not fond of being viewed in the company of witches, I arranged this private assignation."

"If she doesn't like witches, then how does she know your brother?" Marianne inquired, the distrust in her voice evident.

Sage repeated her question, thinking it a competent

one. The tingle on the back of his neck intensified since approaching this woman, warning him of danger. He suspected Marianne felt the same.

"Your brother has traveled extensively in the past," Desmonda explained. "We met during one of his travels. I could go into details if you like, but it is a rather long story. I don't believe we have time for a lengthy discourse. At any moment someone might turn the corner and discover us."

"And you don't wish to be seen with me. I understand."

"I have no particular reason to avoid you, Mr. Merriweather, but you are not the only being capable of acknowledging the dead. I have enemies. I don't wish for anyone with that ability to happen upon me while in the company of your little witch friend who stands at your side."

"I'm not dead," Marianne muttered.

Sage ignored Marianne's disgruntled indignation. Instead, he glanced at her, confused by Miss Green's misidentification of his particular inborn talent.

"Miss Green," he said. "Perhaps you misunderstand. I am a witch, too."

"Oh no, Mr. Merriweather, that you are not. Not any longer. You've bonded with a demon. You carry demon blood."

Chapter Two

Demon...

Sage's blood turned to icc as Desmonda Green's words sank into his brain. Marianne gasped. The skin on his arm grew cold. He recognized the sensation. Marianne touched him.

"Sage?" Marianne whispered, as if she feared Desmonda might overhear her question. "What does she mean?"

He wished to say he didn't know what she spoke of, that the woman must be deranged or made some horrible, *horrible* mistake, that she mistook him for someone else.

The reality was much more grim.

The ringing in his ears prevented him from speaking straightaway. He witnessed Marianne's movements from the corner of his eye as she approached from his side, stepping to face him. Concern and fright glowed from her like a beacon in the dark night.

It made his stomach twist to let Marianne know. Until this moment he'd hidden the truth. He hadn't even told Basil. Basil, his eldest brother, who confided everything to him, who shared his deepest, darkest secrets with Sage, yet Sage could not bring himself to utter a word of his own horrifying experience. It was too terrible to put into words.

His vision narrowed so only Miss Green filled his view. Marianne was not forgotten. Although as a ghost, he sensed her presence as if she held his hand and squeezed. He inhaled deeply, smelling her favorite lavender-scented perfume.

Now was not the time to deal with Marianne's endless curiosity and questions. He'd be happy to postpone that for later. Much later. Tomorrow. No, next week. Perhaps next month.

"How do you know?" His mouth tasted like dust. The mere query he put to Desmonda felt like a confession. Marianne gasped. A dozen sharp daggers pierced his heart. Would she ever speak to him again? Marianne was a witch and a good person. She never condoned evil of any kind, including black magic despite the work practiced on her. A demon was the blackest of magic. She would have none of his help now.

"Did you not know? Demons can smell their kin." A small smile curved Desmonda's lips, like a cat licking spilled cream.

The hairs on the back of his arms stood despite the warm summer air. Instinct screamed to back away, far away from this woman, this…creature.

She's a demon!

He held himself in check. Fear of demons had been pounded into his skull since his childhood. The elders taught children the ways of magic and the world. Whoto trust and who to fear. Demons, of course, topped that second list.

But he would not give in to fear now and allow an opportunity to escape. He and Marianne came seeking information…help. Their journey toward discovering a spell for Marianne neared an end. He knew it. He felt it. Whether her spirit would be reunited with her body or she was doomed to forever roam the world as a ghost, he did not know. All he knew was Desmonda Green might assist them in some way.

"Let us leave," Marianne said her voice a breathy fear-filled whisper. "Now."

"No." Sage forced calm into his voice in an effort to soothe Marianne, even while his innards shook with the same trepidation. "We have questions."

"Someone must know the answers. Let us search elsewhere."

"And if we find no one else?" Sage finally broke eye contact with Desmonda to face Marianne. He expected to detect fear and horror on her lovely features, so it was not surprising to find her eyes open wide, her bottom lip quivering. The desire to wrap his arms around her made him tremble. He wanted to touch her cheek, to wipe away any unseen tears she shed in her distress. To wrap her in the cloak of his embrace and tell her he would protect her from all harm.

It was a promise he could never make.

Marianne was already cursed. Any promise of comfort and safety he might offer came far too late.

And he bore demon blood.

They were both doomed.

"We cannot deal with a demon, Sage. They cannot be trusted."

"Marianne," he said, keeping his voice soft. "We must deal with Miss Green. We have little option available to us."

"Would it ease your mind to know I am not a full-blooded demon?" Desmonda drew their attention back to her. "My mother is human. My powers are not as dark nor as powerful."

"Then how can you help us?"

"I know many people. You'll have to trust me. I understand it will be difficult, but I think you've both gone through enough to allow a little risk."

Sage was about to say something more when Desmonda straightened and placed one finger to her lips to indicate silence.

He listened and soon heard a pair of voices deep in conversation. They were growing closer. In any moment, they would be upon them. There was no place to hide. The alcove Desmonda had chosen was a dead end in the labyrinth, a place to confuse and turn around. Understanding neither wished to be discovered, Sage took several steps closer to Desmonda, only stopping when he stood directly in front of her.

"You'll have to trust us, too," he whispered. "Since I have a feeling there's something you want from us."

He didn't give Miss Green any chance to answer. The owners of the voices were about to turn the corner.

Sage leaned forward, covering the last distance between them. He wrapped his arms around Desmonda and kissed her.

Startled, she tried to pull back, but he held her fast, hoping she understood this was a mere pretense. It took a second or two before she relaxed, lifting her arms to embrace him and tilting her head to better receive his sudden and unexpected kiss.

He listened to the footsteps of the men as they came to a halt behind them. They hesitated a moment, and he knew they were being watched so his hand traveled from Desmonda's neck to the curve of her back. He hesitated only a moment before sliding it lower.

She inhaled and tightened arms around his neck.

The move worked, as the men chuckled at the sight of the lover's embrace. Footsteps continued by without further hesitation.

"They're gone," Marianne whispered. Her voice sounded strained and slightly winded.

He released Miss Green and took a step back, allowing her room for breath while he took a moment to catch his own. Perhaps it was the demon bond he possessed, but his lips felt strange after contact with hers. The urge to wipe his mouth assaulted him, but the rude gesture hardly guaranteed sympathy. He dare not anger this woman before they discovered what she could do for them. But Sage had kissed many women, and although it had been quite some time since his last lover, he found no spark of desire.

Odd. Being a rake, he was well known for seduction. In the past he'd enjoyed it thoroughly. Perhaps Marianne's presence distracted him. He sincerely wished she were not present to witness the kiss. He sensed her standing behind him and wondered at the expression on her face. On second thought, he'd rather not know.

Desmonda darted a look at him before taking a deep shuddering breath. He wondered if she experienced the same bothersome sensation darting into the pit of her stomach.

"We'd better conclude our meeting for tonight. We risk too much to be seen. We'll arrange to meet again under better circumstances to discuss our mutual needs."

The way she spoke the words made Sage cringe. She had no idea about his needs.

"Do you know my London address?" At her nod, he continued, "Send a note explaining where and when you wish to meet. I will be there."

"Agreed."

He nodded in her direction. "It's been a pleasure, Miss Green."

She said nothing as he turned and left. Marianne, who continued to remain strangely silent, followed him. Together they walked, turning left, then right, then left, retracing their footsteps until they found the entrance of the maze.

At the sight of the steps leading to the patio, Sage released a deep breath.

"We have much to discuss, you and I," he said without glancing at Marianne. "I ask to wait until we return home. Then I will answer your questions."

She did not speak which boded ill. Marianne was rarely without words. Reluctant to look at her, he feared the condemnation he might find in her eyes. The kiss he shared with Desmonda still burned on his lips.

Once he reached the top of the steps, he turned pretending to gaze out upon the gardens for those who might notice him. Instead, he faced her. She remained at the bottom of the steps. Her head tilted upward as she watched him, a solemn expression masking the emotions usually so easy to read upon her face.

What was she thinking?

Was she horrified? Did she wish to leave him and return home to her sister, Julia? Did she think him a monster? He carried a demon's bond. He was a monster.

Would she never speak to him again?

Dismay at many of the possible scenarios flashing through his mind kept him from leaping to her side to beg forgiveness. He feared if he moved a muscle in her direction she might flee. So instead, he remained fixed in his position, awaiting her response.

The sounds of the musicians' instruments playing in the ballroom mixed with the general murmur of the couples dancing and those other guests conversing along the edges of the dance floor filled his ears with a low roar. He found it difficult to concentrate.

Knowing the results of potential loss of concentration, he fought to regain it. The back of his hand began to itch and burn. He focused on Marianne, trying to silence his erratic emotions and think only of her.

Her angel-like countenance masked the spirited hellion he knew her to be.

Although their age difference kept them at a distance, Sage recalled little Marianne trailing her older sister at every opportunity. Since their mother's death, Julia had cared for Marianne as if she were her own daughter, creating a bond stronger than most siblings shared.

Suffice it to say, he thought he knew Marianne quite well, but as he studied her, he wondered if he were not mistaken. How well did he truly know her heart and mind?

Marianne tilted her head as she regarded him in turn. He sensed another question stirring her thoughts when her lips parted and her eyes widened. He waited, pretending patience while his heart beat loudly in his ears.

Her reddish-blonde hair formed ringlets around her face. Her blue eyes searched his soul. A dress of white muslin with tiny pink rosebuds covered her thin body. And though she was several inches shorter than his own tall frame, as he regarded her, he thought she stood rather tall compared to most other women of his acquaintance.

She moved, taking slow, measured steps up the stairs. Her thoughtful expression might have given him reason to hope, except for the slight furrow on her delicate brow. She was deep in thought, but she must have come to some sort of decision as she marched toward him.

When she stood before him, he braced himself for her anger, scorn and ire. No doubt the scathing words about to exit her mouth would cut him to the quick. He'd been the target of Marianne's wrath numerous times in the past, but never when he deserved it as mightily as he did in this moment.

She opened her mouth to speak, but no sound emerged. The blood drained from her face, no easy feat for an incorporeal being. Fearing she suffered from some manner of ghostly apoplexy, he tried to reach out to her, only just remembering he could not touch her moments before his hand sliced through her arm. His skin shivered where he made contact with her phantom-being.

His actions managed to snap her out of whatever condition had struck her, for she quickly looked up. Only then did he realize she did not see him, but some object beyond his shoulder in the ballroom.

"Marianne?" He wanted to say more, but it was not necessary. She needed no further prompting.

"He's here." She started into the ballroom. "He's dancing with Charlotte Smythe."

"Who's here?" He moved to look, but she reached to grab him. Her hand struck his shoulder. He felt nothing save a cold blast of air.

"Do not," she scolded and he remained in her direction as she gazed with horror past his shoulder.

"Marianne, who is it?"

"David Fernsby," she said. "My fiancé."

Chapter Three

"You're engaged?"

Marianne didn't respond. For once, words failed her. Instead of answering, she continued staring through the sea of faces focusing on the one that had somehow caught her attention.

David's blond hair shimmered like an angel's halo. He reminded her of an angel. His blue eyes held compassion, tenderness and warmth. His smile was infectious, and his features were perfectly symmetrical. He resembled a masterpiece crafted by an unknown talented artist. She recalled the fluttering that occurred in her belly whenever he spoke to her or danced with her, even looked at her. Her knees would turn to pudding, and her quick-witted tongue would suddenly become tied in knots.

She'd known when she'd first met him, he was the one for her. And only weeks later he claimed her as his forever by offering marriage.

Everyone agreed they were the perfect pair. His wealth and handsomeness matched with her beauty and spirit. Undoubtedly they would produce amazingly talented and beautiful offspring.

"Does he know?" Sage's query dragged her mind back to the present.

"Of course not."

"How have you explained your extended absence?

He must wish to speak with you if you are affianced."

"Julia writes letters for me. Her writing is similar to my own hand, so I dictate, and she posts them."

"He thinks you're in the country? At Merriweather Manor? Why does he not insist on visitations? Does he think you're sick with some contagious disease? After all this time?" Sage's voice was filled with incredulous wonder. Marianne did not doubt his surprise. She told only a select few of her engagement. Her intentions had been to announce their intentions to marry at a ball thrown by his parents, but Drake's machinations cut into those plans. Marianne had to beg off, hoping to postpone until her current dilemma was resolved. How was she to know it would take months, not weeks?

"No, that wouldn't do. The manor is much too close, and he'd offer to visit if I were ill, contagious or not. I did play the part of invalid at first, thinking we had time to convince Drake to reverse the spell. When it became obvious he would not, I told David I was to travel to Bath to take the waters. Days turned weeks, and I could only claim illness for so long before I'd needed to confess my sickness was terminal. I could not have that. So, traveling seemed the best excuse available to me. He thinks I'm abroad, touring the Continent with extended family before I return home to marry him."

"He must be a very patient man to wait so long," Sage remarked.

"He loves me," Marianne said sharply.

"Does he not wonder that all your letters come from England?"

"He believes Julia receives a package containing the letters and then she sends them to him. I had no other way to explain."

Sage's stunned silence drew her attention.

"What else could be done? Telling him the truth was out of the question. He's not a witch."

"What?" Sage's voice rose to such a pitch nearby guests turned to see what he was about. Their eyebrows raised in wonder and curiosity when they realized he stood alone.

"Remember where you are!" Marianne hissed after more people turned to inspect him.

He blinked, and then glanced around. Finding himself the center of attention he strode into the ballroom. Marianne scurried forth before she lost him in the crowded mass of bodies.

"Where are you going?" Marianne shouted above the din created by the music and gossiping crowd.

"Home." He did not verify if she heard, fearing to draw more unwanted attention.

"I'm not leaving," Marianne stated. "Not yet."

He turned, rubbing his hand over his mouth to cover the sight of him talking to air. "We have nothing left here," he mumbled. "All is finished for now."

"No." Marianne shook her head. "I want to see David."

Sage took a deep breath as he regarded her. "It's better we return home. Now."

She shook her head again to add emphasis. "Not for me. I wish to see him. It's been so long since I've seen him."

"I don't think that's wise, Marianne." Sage's voice grew soft as people nearby sent surreptitious glances his way.

"You go," she said, coming to the obvious

conclusion for this argument. "I'll stay a bit. Then I'll return home. It's not like I'm in any danger without an escort. No one can see me, after all. What harm can befall a ghost?"

She thought she heard him groan, but the noise surrounding her made it difficult to be certain.

"I don't wish to find out," he muttered. "Come along, we'll see to your young Fernsby. Then we leave. Together."

"It's not necessary for to you stay," Marianne called as he turned to march toward David. With Sage gone, she'd have ample time to stand beside her beloved. To hear his voice. To watch him dance. To simply be near him again. If Sage left, Marianne had the freedom to spend all night in David's presence. Her heart leapt at the possibility and then fell back down as Sage twisted and turned through the crush of people. There would be no dissuading him now. He would stay by her side. Marianne had no hope of keeping David's company this night.

She sighed, then followed close behind Sage, preferring to walk in his wake rather than make her own way. Being invisible, it was clearly impossible for her to avoid contact with people walking into her. Although neither she nor the person colliding with her came to any harm from the contact, she did feel an otherworldly shiver ice up the spot she touched. It proved rather annoying and slightly uncomfortable if she were honest about it.

"What do you plan to do? Introduce yourself?" The sarcasm slipped easily from Marianne's tongue. Then she gasped. Is that what he intended? Did he plan to reveal the truth? "No, Sage, no! Do not tell him!"

23

He sent her an odd look over his shoulder, one she'd seen a time or two before when she'd done something dimwitted or surprising. With his eyebrow raised, he turned back toward his target.

Marianne held her breath as Sage approached David. He was going to speak to him. Would Sage tell him the truth? That she was a witch, cursed to spend eternity as a phantom? Would David believe him? After all, witches had a reputation for keeping their practices to themselves, what with the burnings and hangings in recent centuries. He might be tempted to suggest Sage visit Bedlam.

But tragic family memories lived long and most witches never spoke of magic abilities to outsiders, human or otherworldly, even though most supernatural beings could sense a fellow creature of magic.

Instead of speaking to David Fernsby, Sage walked past him and stopped in front of a woman standing nearby.

"Mrs. Watson," Sage said, a charming smile lighting his face like a mask during a masquerade. "How lovely to see you again."

"Mr. Merriweather. What a delight!" The spark in the woman's eyes and her matching grin were a clear indication of her pleasure at his approach. "I have not seen you since last Season. Where have you been hiding?"

"A few matters needed my attention, nothing more," he said, keeping the truth vague and dull. Enough to gain interest, Marianne gauged.

She paid no more mind as he began his seduction. After all, that's what he was about. He wanted nothing to do with her or her fiancé. An odd mixture of relief and disappointment flooded her. She stared at Sage as if seeing him for the first time. The image of his kiss with the half-demon flashed in her memory, leaving a sour taste in her mouth.

Where David was an angel of light and love, Sage was his dark counterpart, devilishly handsome with short-cropped dark hair the color akin to mahogany. The blue of his eyes drew many compliments and words of affection. And Sage was outrageously tall while David equaled her own meager height. Marianne often thought she might need a stool if she ever wished to kiss Sage. Not that she wished to. Why would she wish to? It was just a thought, after all.

Not desiring to witness Sage work his seductive wiles over the lovely Mrs. Watson, Marianne centered her attention on David.

He struck a powerful figure while he danced, his back rigid, his steps confident and his smiles radiant. He chatted with his partner during their dance, making Marianne remember all the conversations they shared while dancing and in between sets.

A waltz.

It would be a waltz, Marianne mused. They were Fernsby's favorites, as well as her own. It gave them every excuse to hold each other close together, to whisper words of love without the fear of being overheard by chaperones.

Only now, David's left hand firmly clasped Charlotte Smythe's hand instead of hers. His right hand cradled Charlotte's body, caressing like a lover's touch. The sight struck pain into her chest, but she rallied knowing David could never love Charlotte Smythe. No doubt he felt compelled to ask her to dance, the poor girl. She was rather homely in appearance.

Marianne tried to take her thoughts away from Charlotte and instead studied David.

He looked well, as always.

The music's last notes echoed. The dance ended. David and Charlotte parted, bowing to each other in respect until David straightened, placing Charlotte's hand on his elbow. Then they walked hand on arm toward the open French doors leading to the patio and garden.

Marianne started to follow them. She took two steps when a loud gasp of fright ignited the air behind her. She spun, startled to discover Sage's hand engulfed in flame and burning like a torch.

****

Sage's attempts to engage in flirtatious conversation normally came so naturally. He developed the talent over years of living in London, often using it to his advantage. The ton often referred to him as the Merriweather Rake since he was the most charming and charismatic of his brothers. But in this instance, his attention kept wandering to Marianne looking so forlorn at the edge of the dance floor while that young pup wooed the girl in his arms. Sage recognized the signs of seduction. As soon as the music ended, he had no doubt Fernsby planned to escort the young lady out to the garden to take in the fresh air while gazing at the moonlight. A few whispered words, a few innocent caresses, one thing leading to another, and next he'd be passionately kissing her in one of the dark alcoves of the hedge labyrinth. If they found a great deal of privacy, perhaps more than simple kissing would be involved…

And Marianne would witness it.

Every bit of it.

How to stop her?

Sage could try to say something. She wouldn't listen. As a ghost, Marianne remained every bit as stubborn as when she had been human. He could interfere in Fernsby's plans, perhaps intercept them, ask Miss Smythe to dance. Imagining the look on Marianne's face while Sage danced with the same woman swayed him from the notion. It would pain her to see this woman getting so much attention from the men in her life. Besides, Fernsby would waste no time moving on to another young lady. Could Sage follow the scoundrel throughout every dance, intercepting every young lady while Marianne watched on?

The best thing to do was get Marianne out of here, far away from Fernsby until he could decide what must be done with him. It could be Sage was jumping to conclusions. Perhaps Fernsby was a gentleman of known repute, someone admired and respected. Sage glanced again at the man in question, noticing the man's gaze fixed on Miss Smythe's ample cleavage where it remained for the rest of the dance.

Did Marianne not see this?

Sage looked at her, viewing her profile. The yearning on her face, the love shining in her eyes, the sadness at her inability to be with this man proved to Sage that she was not aware of Fernsby's faults. She saw him in the best light.

Anger surged through Sage. How could Fernsby do this to Marianne? Did he not know how she loved him? How much she desired to be with him? It was written plainly on her features. Even if he forgot for a moment that Marianne was invisible to all, the fury still consumed him. He wished nothing more than to call young Fernsby out to teach him a lesson about love and self-sacrifice. Marianne deserved far better.

Then Mrs. Watson screamed.

His attention jerked back to her, not realizing how consumed he'd been in watching the scene of Marianne and her beau play out before him.

At first he did not know why the woman screamed. She gaped at him in horror. What had he done?

"Your hand, sir! Your hand!" A man standing next to him shouted, stepping closer to splash liquid contained in a glass over Sage's hand.

A stinging, burning sensation hit. Sage looked at his hand. Red and orange flames licked his skin. He jumped, alarmed to discover his appendage indeed on fire. Quickly, he shimmied out of his evening jacket, using the black cloth to tamp down the flames.

A dozen or more people crowded around him pleased the fire had not spread. Fortunately no one had shouted about the fire, or there might have been a stampede of ballroom occupants toward the nearest exits. Many people might have been seriously injured or killed in this crush.

"I'm fine. I'm fine," he repeated, with each question shouted about his welfare.

"Damned candles. You must have brushed your sleeve over one. We must see to your hand, sir." The man who attempted the rescue by splashing his drink spoke. He was a gentleman near Sage's age, with kind eyes and a ready smile. The man looked vaguely familiar, but Sage could not place him. "I can have the finest physician check you over, if you'll just come this way. Ladies, do not fear. Mr. Merriweather will be right as rain."

"I'm fine," Sage kept saying. His shocked brain could barely register anything else. He was nowhere near any candles, standing far enough from tables or sconces while he stood near the edge of the dancing. It was not possible that he brushed against any candles.

The only way this might have happened was if he'd cast a spell. But he hadn't. Had he?

Was it possible? Had his power created the fire? Without using any spells?

"Sage! Sage!"

Marianne.

He glanced up realizing only then that he crouched on the tiled ballroom floor. The crowd of concerned onlookers leaned over him, and his chest tightened. Suddenly, he was short of breath. His chest heaved, gasping for air.

"Marianne." He could barely hear the sound of his voice against the roar of the crowd as they all spoke at once.

"Mr. Merriweather, what can we do to assist you?"

"My dear, did you see his arm?"

"It was his hand."

"On fire! He's lucky Lord Valentine doused it in time."

"Mr. Merriweather, such a terrible tragedy! Do you think there will be excessive scarring?"

"He may never regain the use of his hand."

"It was his arm."

On and on the voices rattled until his teeth set on edge, and he could feel a roar begin to rumble in his chest.

"Come, Mr. Merriweather," Lord Valentine urged, his hand extended. "Let's get you someplace where we can better examine you."

"Marianne," he said in response. Sage's vocabulary hadn't improved. He'd gone from *I'm fine* to calling, *Marianne*.

Had he imagined Marianne's voice calling to him moments ago? Where was she? Had she abandoned him to follow Fernsby? His thoughts centered on her, worries overshadowing the dilemma he faced with this crowd. He needed to find her before she discovered Fernsby was not the devoted fiancé she imagined.

"Yes, we will find your Miss Marianne," Lord Valentine said calmly. "I'm certain she is fine. Ladies, if you could please step back. The poor man needs some air. Come now, ladies, we can't allow Mr. Merriweather to expire from your smothering attentions."

Loud giggles erupted, but with a little more urging, a gap in the crowd emerged.

"Sage!" Marianne appeared in the opening, rushing toward him only to back away when someone else moved into her path. She didn't like being touched by the corporeal. That's why she hadn't come to his side.

He breathed a sigh of relief. She hadn't gone after Fernsby. She stayed instead.

She stayed.

Lord Valentine's strong fingers wrapped around Sage's upper arm, giving him a lift to his feet. Sage tried to take the burden of his weight off of the other man's shoulders, but Lord Valentine refused to budge from his stance as rescuer.

Sage stood, cradling his injured hand in his ruined

evening jacket. He yearned to wriggle his fingers, but feared what he might experience as a result. So, he held his hand very still and allowed Lord Valentine to lead him out of the ballroom. The music had silenced as even the musicians craned their necks above their instruments to glimpse the commotion. Soft murmurs erupted as he walked by the gaping crowd.

Lord Valentine waved to someone, and a moment later music again filled the ballroom.

Oddly, Sage was not stricken by the attention he received. The old Sage might have reveled in it, knowing by tonight he'll receive dozens or more letters and notes from the beautiful women in attendance, all asking after his welfare and declaring their hope that if they might do anything to ease his pain or assist in his speedy recovery he need only mention it. And of course, he would.

Yes, the old Sage would have leapt at the opportunities available to him.

That Sage was gone, however. Now he wished only to quit the room, leave the house and return to the comfort and safety of his own home.

With Marianne.

He spared a glance to his left, relieved to find her following at a discreet distance so as not to come into contact with anyone. Her brow furrowed, and she bit her bottom lip. She caught sight of his gaze, and he spared a smile for her. She smiled back, relief easing the stress of her worry.

"Would you kindly have one of the footmen call for my carriage, my lord," Sage said once they exited the ballroom.

"Let us see to your hand first, Mr. Merriweather.

You might be in no condition for a lengthy drive home."

"I'm quite all right." Sage wanted to leave, before anything else went wrong. "It appeared more startling than it truly was."

"I'll be the judge of that. I insist. We'll need to bandage it until a physician can attend to it."

"I appreciate your concern, my lord, but I assure you all is well. I simply wish to go home. My jacket is ruined," he said at an attempt at humor.

"I beg your pardon, sir, but I could not in good conscience allow you to leave this house without offering some sort of medical assistance. You must be in a great deal of pain. What if you lose consciousness while you're driving?"

"That won't happen."

"It won't if you allow me to tend it."

"Sage, he's not going to relent. Lord Valentine is known for being more stubborn than I am, I can assure you. And perhaps it is best if he at least bandages it. You don't want blood staining your carriage seats, do you?"

Sage regarded her for a moment. She still worried, despite the light-hearted tone she used. Since he didn't wish to argue any longer, Sage nodded his consent. Lord Valentine sent servants to fetch clean cloth for bandages, then he urged him into the study where they could sit without a crowd of people overwhelming them.

"Here." Lord Valentine gestured to the chair beside the mahogany desk that took up most of the room. "Do you care for a glass of sherry? Perhaps something stronger?"

"No, thank you," Sage said as he sat. He glanced around the room, remembering why Lord Valentine looked so familiar. He was his host.

"Very well, let's get right to it then, shall we?"

Lord Valentine leaned over Sage and helped him carefully unwrap the evening jacket away from his hand. When at last, his hand was free of the confines of dark cloth, Lord Valentine gasped. He lifted Sage's hand, turning it over to inspect the skin.

"I saw it engulfed in flames, and yet..." Lord Valentine whispered in disbelief. "There isn't a mark, not even a scratch to prove it."

Sage flexed his fingers, inspecting the skin alongside Lord Valentine.

Just as he feared.

"It must have been a trick of the light," Sage said, offering an alternative, something to explain the unexplainable.

"But, look here, at the cuff of your sleeve. It is singed. There most definitely was a fire that burned your sleeve. Why did it not touch your skin?"

"You were quick to douse it, my lord," Sage said, trying a smile at yet another alternative.

Lord Valentine released Sage's hand and leaned back, resting against the edge of his desk.

"I've never seen the like." He stared at Sage in wonder.

Sage needed to get out of here. Too many questions needed answering. Even Marianne stood by the fire, silenced by the sight of his hand. How could he explain it? Even witches burned. History could attest to that.

Demons, however, were a different story. And

apparently that included witches cursed by demons.

"I must go, my lord. I feel fatigued from all this."

"Then perhaps you should stay. I can have the servants ready another guest room."

"I thank you for your kind offer, but I must return to town. I have business that cannot be postponed."

Lord Valentine stared for a long moment, studying him as if judging whether it would be prudent to confine him against his will. He might refuse to let Sage go. No one would dare say a word against this man. He was wealthy and powerful and known for his generosity. It would be expected that Lord Valentine keep the man who caught fire in his ballroom until a physician arrived to look over his wounds. In the meantime, Sage could be interrogated over and over again, and no one would be the wiser.

Sage calmed his racing heart, trying to keep focused instead of letting fear get the better of him.

This must be how his ancestors felt when caught in questionable circumstances. Although there hadn't been a public witch trial involving burnings or hangings for any number of years, Sage knew witch-hunters still searched the world to eradicate his kind. They simply did it in other ways that did not garner as much attention, since public opinion had swayed in recent years. And unlike other supernatural creatures that witches could sometimes identify on sight, witch-hunters were very human and blended in with the rest of humanity. Sometimes, the only way to know if a man was a witch-hunter was when it proved too late.

A soft scratching at the door drew Sage's attention from Lord Valentine. A housemaid entered carrying a handful of clean cloth. She deposited the items on the desk where her master bade and left quickly as he ordered.

Lord Valentine lifted a piece of cloth from the pile, opening the square and then folding it again.

"I suppose these are not necessary now, are they?"

Sage shook his head, clenching the fingers of his supposedly wounded hand as if embarrassed he should not have need of them. Foolish, really. Sage wished his hand had been burned. He wished he felt the pain of a wound instead of receiving looks of distrust and accusation.

"Well," Lord Valentine said with a deep sigh. "I'd prefer you stay the night, for my own peace of mind, but as we both can see no physical damage has been done, I'll have the servants bring your carriage round. I would appreciate, however, one day if you are ever able to offer the truth instead of vague fabrications, I would be pleased to hear it."

Sage glanced at Marianne in time to witness her shoulders sag with relief. Her thoughts must have journeyed the same witch-hunter path as his, only she was wise enough not to mention it while in the presence of their host. No need for Sage to appear mad by speaking to thin air, as well as enchanted.

"I do appreciate it, my lord," Sage said humbly. He did not respond to the promise portion of Lord Valentine's statement. He could not conceivably foresee a time at any point in the future where he would feel the need to tell this man the truth about his family. In fact, few knew the Merriweather family secret. Most of their neighbors in Meryton were fellow witches able to cast spells and other enchantments. They kept their secrets close.

Chapter Four

The inside of the carriage filled with noise of the wheels turning over a dirt-packed road. The sounds of nocturnal creatures echoed in the surrounding pastures and forests as they passed by on the way home from Lord Valentine's house party.

Marianne quietly stewed as she watched the trees and brush glide by while Sage handled the reins of the phaeton. It had been a little worrisome when she first boarded his carriage as the horse sensed her presence and did not appreciate a ghost sitting in the vehicle.

Every so often Marianne glanced in Sage's direction, trying to decipher his mood or sense his thoughts. He continued to stare straight ahead, his attention never straying from the road. Several times she attempted speech, but words failed her, a new habit she was beginning to loathe.

What could she say?

She saw the scene unfold again and again.

His hand engulfed in bright orange and yellow flames, burning from his wrist to fingertips. And then in Lord Valentine's private study, the gentle and careful unwrapping to reveal the smooth skin of an unharmed hand.

Marianne still had difficulty believing her eyes. She wished to touch his hand, to feel the smooth skin with her own fingers, to know for herself that he was truly uninjured.

It was both a blessing and a curse that she had not the ability to touch him.

She tilted her head to the side, looking again at his hand while it gripped the reins. Though he now wore gloves, she felt as though she could see through the soft leather to the skin beneath. There were no scars. How could there be no scars? No burnt flesh, no blood oozing from broken or ravaged skin. Not even any redness.

How?

"Would you care to see it again?" His deep voice rumbled in the darkness. "It remains unchanged, I assure you."

"I… Forgive me. Staring is impossibly rude. How unfair am I to—"

"Do you fear me?"

Marianne turned to face him fully, surprised by the scorn she detected.

"Of course not!"

"Then…what?"

"I do not comprehend." Marianne chose her words carefully. "The absence of any wound warrants an explanation. I fear you will not confide in me."

"Why would I refuse?"

"Because I'm simply Marianne," she said torn between bitterness and sarcasm. "Julia Grey's younger sister whom she treats as more of a reckless child than a sibling. How often am I kept in the dark concerning matters of import, even when those matters regard me? You and Basil have your secrets. Julia and Basil keep their own. I have no secrets. Not any longer. Everyone knows what's wrong with me."

"There is nothing wrong with you," Sage remarked, glancing at her, surprised by her outburst.

"Oh?" Marianne raised an eyebrow. "Other than having no substance. My spirit won't stay in my body. I can be seen and heard by only three people in this world, two are unable to help me, the third unwilling. I have a fiancé who I must lie to, and my closest friend in this world is keeping secrets from me. Yes, you are right. Nothing wrong with me at all."

She regretted her outburst as soon as the last syllable spilled from her mouth.

"Closest friend? Do you mean your sister? Why would she keep secrets from you?" Sage said, narrowing on the one point she wished he had not heard.

She said nothing at first. Instead, she looked off into the distance, wanting to pretend nothing was spoken. She'd uttered too much already.

"Julia is your closest friend, yes?"

"Julia is my sister," Marianne snapped, again regretting her outburst.

"Then who is your closest friend? Surely not Basil. Since he left when you were so young, I can't imagine you remember much of him from your childhood."

"Can we not move on in our discussion?" Marianne suggested, growing impatient with his guesses.

He fell silent. Marianne was pleased he had chosen not to pursue this particular line of questioning.

"Aunt Petunia?"

She sighed, dramatically for effect. He was the most annoying and exasperating man. And stubborn. Almost as stubborn as she but perhaps more patient.

Her own patience had grown thin.

"*You* are, you twit!"

She resumed her study of geography, wishing they might arrive at Merriweather Manor at any moment. She wanted to go home.

Being a ghost hadn't liberated her from movement or travel. She couldn't flash from one location to another in the blink of an eye as she wished. She'd tried. Instead, she needed corporeal transport or the ability of her own two feet to walk the lane home, a prospect she found both dull and tedious. At least on a carriage, she'd have people to listen to, faces to look at and a way to entertain herself. Walking was a dreary business, one she'd rather not participate in, spirit or not.

And spells were beyond her powers. Even incantations were ineffective. The talent she had as a witch had vanished, along with all hope of returning to her body. She could still sense magic, but beyond that her skills were useless.

"Marianne, I—"

"Please don't speak," she said. "Unless you plan to offer some explanation for the series of events this evening, I'd rather simply watch the scenery."

"Marianne…"

She sighed again. Of course he wouldn't let her sit in peace. He would pursue this until she answered all of his questions while he answered none of hers.

Thunder boomed and a flash of light appeared on the road directly in front of them, jolting her attention. The horse whinnied in fright, swerving to pull off the road. Sage nearly stood in his seat to regain control, but after a second crash of thunder, this time coming from behind, he loosened the reins, allowing the horse freedom to run.

If Marianne had any substance, she would have fallen back in the seat at the pace he set.

"Get down!" Sage yelled, which was a pointless endeavor, but she chose not to remind him.

"What's happening?" she shouted, as another boom of thunder broke through the darkness. This time, she recognized the sound for what it was…gunpowder exploding from a pistol or musket.

"Ambush!" Sage shouted back.

She gasped, wishing she could cling to the seats. She had difficulty breathing for a moment as he raced the phaeton down the dusty lane that would eventually lead to a coaching inn. Although Sage had told her he hoped to press on until London, he knew the darkening sky would not assist him, despite the full moon illuminating the landscape.

The full moon apparently assisted their attackers since the accuracy had improved with each shot.

A buzzing filled Marianne's ears. Her shoulder tingled and burned as though someone touched it. It happened again an instant later lower in her chest. It took her a moment to realize those were bullets passing through her spirit form. If her body had sat in its place, she would be dead.

Sage grunted and flinched, grabbing his arm, then releasing it to grab at the reins again.

"Damned highwaymen!" He growled as he regained control. The carriage careened to the left. Marianne closed her eyes when the carriage tipped to the side, certain they would topple over. Somehow, the carriage righted itself. Marianne blinked open her eyes.

"Where are they?" Sage shouted. "Damn, where are they?"

Marianne looked up to see Sage pulling a pistol from a hidden compartment beneath his seat. He was having difficulty handling the reins and holding the weapon at the same time.

She opened her mouth to tell him to hand over the pistol. He had taught her to shoot and claimed she was a superb markswoman, but as she lifted her hand to offer help she remembered. How could she forget? She couldn't help him. Although she sat next to Sage, conversing with him as a normal human would, she was all but dead. A ghost. He was alone, being chased by highwaymen on a dark country road.

There was no one to help him.

Tears blurred her vision as she looked back to find two riders on horseback emerge from the darkness at the side of the road. When it became clear Sage did not plan to stop the carriage despite their deadly warning, they pushed into pursuit.

"What can I do?" Marianne whispered to herself.

The highwaymen continued firing. Marianne didn't bother cowering with fright since the bullets that struck her did no injury. She could stand on the back of this phaeton, it would make no difference. She was useless and would remain so until she had her body back. She couldn't even reveal herself in an effort to scare them.

"That's it!" Marianne shouted. She knew how to help.

"What?"

With no time to respond, she closed her eyes to concentrate on something tugging her downward, an energy source that pulled her through the seat of the carriage and onto the road.

"Marianne!"

She heard his startled cry but refused to answer. She hit the ground and stood to face the oncoming riders. Holding her arms out in front of her, she waited for the horses, welcoming them as they neared. Just as she suspected, both horses reared when they drew close, fighting against their masters as they refused to go near her. The horses sensed and feared her.

Foul language spilled from the rider's mouths as they fought to regain control of the animals. The horses refused until one managed to step around her. She tried to intercept it, but he was too quick. Again, he continued the chase.

Marianne watched him go, disappointed she hadn't held him at a bay longer, but satisfied she gave Sage a chance to widen the gap between him and his pursuers.

The second horse and its rider stepped around her while she was distracted.

Sage's phaeton grew smaller in the distance. Marianne hoped he might outrun them. The only course left to her now was to walk.

Just as she resigned herself to a night of haunting a long stretch of English countryside road, she heard a groaning creak ahead. The phaeton tilted. It smashed onto its side, flipping into the ditch at the side of the road.

Chapter Five

"*Marianne!*" Sage searched frantically, finding nothing save empty space beside him. His heart pounded so loudly he no longer heard the gunfire.

She had vanished. Slipped through the cushions on the seat and vanished. He hadn't even known she was capable of such a thing. Where had she gone? There weren't many places she could hide in his phaeton. He prayed wherever she went was safe. And when he saw her again, he would give her the longest and most fierce lecture of his career.

The fright the woman gave him!

He fought to control the horse. His shirt was soaked with blood. He'd been shot in the arm during the gunfire, but didn't have time to examine the severity of the wound. Instead, he focused on outrunning the highwaymen who suddenly seemed to have fallen behind. The horse's hooves grew distant.

He was about to offer a prayer of thanks to the gods when he slammed backward, falling into his seat. Pain scorched his shoulder. Gunfire echoed. Ahead, a lone rider, stood with a pistol pointed in his direction.

How had the highwayman gotten in front of him?

"Damn," Sage muttered, grasping his shoulder.

He'd been shot.

Again.

Another groan, this time coming from the carriage.

The creaking of the wheels sent panic through him. The wheel was cracking. The phaeton jerked, bounced. Sage pulled on the reins in an attempt to slow the horse before the wheel snapped. With a broken wheel, the phaeton could crash and do the horse injury. Not to mention himself. But the panicked horse refused to slow. If anything, he picked up speed.

"No, no, no," Sage muttered. His carriage drew closer to the rider who hadn't budged from his spot on the road ahead.

He heard the loud smash as the wheel snapped, then the carriage tipped. This was it. He was going to crash. With only a moment to think of what must be done, Sage leapt from his seat, falling into the foliage. His feet hit the ground first, then his legs crumpled. The force of momentum rolled him down a ditch. His knee hit a rock, and blinding pain ran along his leg.

Yet another injury to add to the rest.

When he came to a stop at the bottom of the ditch, he lifted his head. The carriage had fallen to its side. The wheel shattered into pieces. The horse was down and scrambling viciously to get free, the sounds of its panic clawing at his heart. He needed to free the horse. If the horse wasn't already injured, he surely would be while he fought for freedom.

First, Sage needed to get out of the ditch. In his condition, it didn't seem a likely prospect. His shoulder and side burned like fire. He hadn't even looked at his knee.

Horse's hooves thundered on the dirt from both directions of the road.

Add to that, he had highwaymen to consider.

Sage's hand went to grip the pistol and found

nothing but air. It must have dropped during his fall.

With the darkening twilight, bright moonlight lit the ground. He searched the ground nearby for his weapon. If he couldn't find it, he'd be forced to resort to spells and lately his spells were more apt to go awry.

Ever since the demon…

Not now.

Find the pistol. Contend with these highwaymen. And discover where in bloody hell Marianne had gotten.

The rider who appeared in front reached his horse and the remainder of his carriage. He jumped down and started unhitching the horse. When it was no longer leashed to the broken skeleton of his carriage, the horse leapt and galloped off down the road, vanishing into the dark.

At least the horse wasn't injured.

Sage grimaced. He still must deal with the highwaymen. He gave up his search for the pistol. It was nowhere in sight. He focused on the approaching men, one on foot, the other two on horseback.

The man on foot sauntered over and leaned over the ditch. He wore a long leather jacket. When he stopped above him, Sage noticed mud covering his boots.

"Looks like ye're in a pickle," Muddy Boots said. "How's about we get ye outta there and up ta the road where we can talk a piece. Real pleasant like?"

The other men drew the horses to the side of the road.

"Is he dead?" This man's voice sounded refined, educated compared to Muddy Boots. A gentleman's voice.

"Nah, he ain't dead. Yet."

"No killing. You were told no killing."

"I ain't killed him yet, have I?" Muddy Boots retorted, with a disdainful glare at the Gentleman.

"You shot him," the Gentleman observed. "There's blood on his shirt."

"Dirt there, too. Did I scruff him up some? No, I haven't. He lost control of the horse, tipped 'er over and there he lay. What have I to do with it?"

"You shot at him!"

"You was shooting, too."

"Into the air, to frighten him into stopping. I should have known he wouldn't scare easily. The fool."

"Then ye should have known I was gonna shoot him," Muddy Boots haughtily declared with a grin on his weather-beaten face.

Muddy Boots and the silent one hadn't bothered to hide their faces. That did not bode well for Sage. But the Gentlemen had a piece of cloth wrapped around his nose and mouth, cloaking his features so only his eyes were visible.

"Get him up here so we might question him." The Gentleman waved his pistol in Sage's direction.

Muddy Boots and his friend scrambled down into the ditch where they found him ready. As soon as Muddy Boots came within reach, Sage drew back and struck with all his might. His fist connected with the outlaw's cheek. Muddy Boots fell back, landing loudly on his back.

The Silent One backed away, cautious after seeing what was done to his partner. Sage hoped the man was impetuous. He prepared to fight, despite the wounds. His shoulder and leg continued to throb.

The Gentleman came to the side of the ditch. "Why cause yourself more injury? Let my men help you to the road where we can talk."

Something about the voice teased his memory. He knew this man. He didn't recognize the other two, but the Gentleman kept hidden making Sage suspect he knew his identity.

"What do you want?" He'd had a long, tiring night. He wanted to go home, take a bath and go to bed, without a woman for once since all he could think of at the moment was sleep. He was tired, drained, in pain and confused. If these men wished to kill him, he suspected they would have done so already.

"To talk, nothing more," the Gentleman said.

Muddy Boots scrambled to his feet, swaying for a moment as he clasped his jaw.

The Silent One, grabbed Sage's right arm and hauled him up, dragging him. Sage attempted to assist only to gasp when his knee gave out beneath him. Eventually, the men pulled him out and he lay on the road, gasping for breath. He felt like he'd been beaten already.

Torture at this point seemed unnecessary.

"We have one question for you, and then we will leave you in peace," the Gentleman said, kneeling down beside Sage. "Where is the girl, Marianne Grey?"

Out of every query they might have posed, Sage had not anticipated this one. Why did they want to learn of Marianne's whereabouts? At this moment, even he didn't know for certain where she had gone. Her spirit, leastways.

"I don't know," he answered with a shake of his head.

"Get him up," the Gentleman ordered. The other two grabbed his arms, yanking him to his feet. He bit back a cry from the pain in his shoulder. For a moment it felt like Muddy Boots was about to rip his arm free. How big was the hole in his arm? He wiggled his fingers, testing them. He still had feeling and mobility, which was a good sign.

"Grab his hands!" the Gentleman shouted, surging forward to clasp Sage's wrist. "Get the rope. Tie his hands so his fingers have no movement."

"Why the bloody hell would we do that?"

"Because you fool, you're ordered to," the Gentleman said, growling. "This man possesses certain abilities that we must protect ourselves against. Strap him to the carriage wheel."

At first Sage struggled, but he grew weaker with every punch to the gut Muddy Boots used to convince him to submit. He was wounded and in no condition to fight back.

It alarmed him further to realize the Gentleman knew about Sage's magic. He knew he was a witch.

They wrapped the rope around his fingers so Sage could cast no spells. The man didn't know Sage had no intentions to use any spells. He was uncertain if he could cast properly. Until he found a way to free himself from the demon's bond, he had little choice in the matter of protecting himself. He never practiced black magic, in fact he abhorred it. These days even the simplest spells came out wrong, sometimes with near deadly results. Sage would not risk anyone's lives. Not even these scoundrels.

Once they strapped him to the tilted carriage wheel, he reclined across the spokes. The Gentleman stepped forward to stand over him.

"We'll try this again, with no hand movements this time. Where is Marianne Grey's body?"

Her body? They knew her body and spirit were separated.

"Who are you?" Sage asked, trying not to cry out in pain. His arm tilted behind his back at such an angle his injury felt as if it were being torn from his body.

"My name does not matter."

A large hat covered the man's head. The only feature available to view were his eyes. It was difficult to decipher the color in the pale moonlight, but Sage might guess they were blue.

Sage supposed his identity wasn't truly important. It was the man's task that was the issue.

And he knew who was behind it.

"You tell Drake that he will never get to Marianne again. And if he tries to obtain another 'test subject' we will know of it and will stop him. His experimentations are finished."

"Who the hell is Drake?" Muddy Boots asked.

"Quiet, you fool," the Gentleman snapped, giving Sage a measured look.

Sage knew the man's thoughts just by his eyes.

How much pain could Sage endure before he revealed the truth?

Sage might have answered no amount of pain inflicted would match what he'd already suffered. No one knows pain until they are tortured by a demon.

Something caught Sage's awareness beyond the cluster of highwaymen. He focused on the darkness of the road where he had just crashed and saw a woman running. Her dress became clear first, a white frock he recognized instantly.

Marianne!

Sage nearly spoke her name aloud, but caught himself in time. No need to alert this man to the fact that he could speak with the very Marianne he was searching for.

Well, her spirit.

"Sage!" Marianne gasped when she finally drew near enough to be heard. "Are you all right? What have these monsters done to you? What do they want?"

Sage raised an eyebrow, then glanced at each man in a pointed manner.

"Right. *Right.*" Marianne walked around them, scanning each man from head to boot as if she hoped to identify one. "You cannot speak. I understand."

The horses whinnied from where the men tied the reins around branches of nearby trees.

The Gentleman turned suddenly in Marianne's direction. She jumped at his sudden movement. Sage's heart leapt to his throat.

Did he know she was there? Did he *see* her?

The Gentleman stared for a moment and during that time Sage did not take a breath. It seemed to go on forever. At last, the man simply shivered.

"What's wrong?"

"I'm not certain," the man said. "I feel as though someone watches me."

The other two swiveled their heads, searching the moonlit night, looking for any sign of movement along the tree line or at the far end of the road.

"I don't see nobody."

"Nor do I," the man said, then turned back to Sage. Sage could tell he smiled by the way the cloth crinkled around his cheekbones. "She's here, is she not?"

"Who?" Muddy Boots asked.

The Silent One glanced nervously between the two men.

The Gentleman ignored his fellow highwaymen.

"I know she's here. I can sense her presence."

Sage tried not to reveal how much that statement affected him. How it disturbed him to know this man could sense her proximity. It made Marianne vulnerable. The man could do nothing to harm her, but the fact that he sensed her felt akin to...*touching* her. That was something Sage would never allow another man to do.

"I don't know what you're talking about," Sage muttered, glowering at the man, challenging him.

"I have something to try if I should come upon her," the man said. As he spoke he drew a leather pouch from his pocket. Opening the pouch, he emptied the contents into the palm of his hand. It was a white powdery substance. Then he turned in a circle, pausing every so often.

"What is this?" Marianne asked, taking a step closer for a better look.

The man lifted the powder to his mouth and blew. A puff of white billowed into a shimmery cloud aimed directly at Marianne's face. She screamed and fell back clutching her eyes.

"Marianne!" Sage roared, tugging at the ropes that kept him bound.

The man laughed. "I knew I sensed her presence!"

Sage ignored the man's laughter and continued to work at the ropes. It made little difference. He couldn't help Marianne. He couldn't touch her. What could he do other than speak to her?

"What are you goin' on about now?" Muddy Boots asked, clearly having difficulty following the conversation between prisoner and jailer.

Again, the Gentleman did not answer his comrade, merely directed his attention at the emptiness in front of him.

"Ah!" the Gentleman said, the grin crinkling the cloth over his face. He glanced at Sage, his eyes bright and twinkling in the moonlight. "She's very pretty."

At first, Sage did not comprehend. There was no woman other than Marianne. And since it was not possible that he could actually *see* her, then he must be speaking of someone else.

Sage remained silent as the man stepped toward the crumpled form of Marianne. Sage's hands clenched and his fingers flexed with the urge to do spell work. Perhaps something to knock the man off his feet. But he couldn't do it with his fingers bound. The man stepped closer, until he stopped and knelt next to her.

Muddy Boots and the Silent One gasped.

"Where the bloody hell did she come from?" Muddy Boots asked and then cursed. The Silent One crossed himself, which only angered Muddy Boots. "What did you get us into, Roy? This job better pay well! I've got little ones to feed, and I don't want my soul going to Hell because some sort of enchantress appearin' on the side o' the road."

Marianne continued to clutch her face, so she didn't know the man sat beside her until he touched her hair. She jumped and let out a squeal.

Then the man touched her cheek. Marianne swatted at him and wriggled away. She swiped at her eyes, blinking against the powder painted across her skin.

The Gentleman looked directly at Marianne.

"This can't be happening," she whispered, her eyes wide with disbelief.

"Are you not overjoyed, my dear? How long has it been since you've last enjoyed the touch of flesh on flesh?" He reached out again, this time to offer his hand to her so she might stand.

She lifted her arm hesitantly. The man's hands clasped her fingers. She cried out in pleasure, surprise and relief. The emotions danced across her features.

"Is this a dream?" she asked, tilting her head to gape at him.

"No, my sweet," he said, touching her chin.

The sight of the man touching her sickened Sage. His muscles bunched. He strained against the ropes. Even the pain in his shoulder was forgotten as he fought to be free.

He needed to help Marianne. He needed to place himself between Marianne and this highwayman.

And why was she gazing upon this masked man as if he were the knight in shining armor come to rescue her from the evil fire-breathing dragon.

That particular image angered him.

Because it was true, was it not?

Sage had been searching for a spell to reverse the curse, something…*anything* that would help Marianne. For months he searched, reading every spell book he could get his hands on, asking every witch, sorcerer, enchantress, druid and shaman he could find. He even had a vampire and a werewolf assist him in the search.

Yet they found nothing. Not a reference to any sort of spell, not a mention in any book or legend.

Nothing.

Until this man literally yanked the carriage out from beneath their feet, reveals a powder and suddenly all is well.

Marianne…flesh and blood. This *Gentleman* is the hero.

And Sage is still the fire-breathing monster.

The irony in the situation shook him, so much so he didn't realize until that moment how much it mattered.

Ever since the day he walked into Merriweather Manor to discover Marianne cursed with no one to see her save for him and her sister.

He felt there was a reason for it.

A reason he had the ability to see her and no one, not even Basil whose spell power was so much greater than his own, could do the same. Sage had mattered to someone. Someone needed him, well and truly needed him, and he would do anything to help her.

But he had failed.

Fury raged beneath his skin, flexing his muscles until they burned with heat. He stared at the man's fingers, stroking Marianne's chin, leaning toward her…*was he about to kiss her*? Yes, the man was going to kiss her.

The sight enraged Sage. Marianne was not this man's woman to kiss. He had no right.

And she didn't even blink, simply gazed back at the stranger with adoration. *A stranger*!

A stranger who had shot him!

Twice!

The heat burned beneath the skin of his shoulder blades, running up his neck and down his back. He shivered from the delicious intensity. His anger fed the fire in his blood, burning with the need to destroy…something…anything…this man who dared to touch his Marianne.

His Marianne!

Sage's hands felt warm, the heat rising against his palms. If only he dared to cast a spell. But he needed his hands free to do so. If only he could burn through the bonds trapping him with the heat glowing in his blood, then he might wrap those hands around this highwayman's neck. He would delight in watching the man's eyes grow round with horror. He would revel in the gurgling sound as he choked for breath. He yearned to feel bones snap and witness the spark of life leave the man's eyes to grow dull with emptiness.

Suddenly, Sage's hands were free. The ropes smoking and charred, the ends burning bright with flame, fell to his feet. The wheel holding Sage aloft sizzled and snapped. Sage slid from the embers, his feet landing with a thud onto the road.

He roared with pleasure at his sudden freedom. A spark of flame jumped from his skin, lighting the rest of the carriage in a blast of fire as if an explosion hit. The carriage lit like a dry patch of meadow grass, the flames flaring up and licking at the night sky.

The two highwaymen standing to the side screamed. Sage growled and cast a fireball in their direction as they turned and ran. His aim was off and it landed at their feet. The frightened horses whinnied and reared, then galloped down the road, abandoning their masters who scrambled after them. Sage considered following, but turned instead to the man who held Marianne captured against his chest.

The man used her as a shield while backing slowly away. Marianne's face became a blur. Sage didn't even look at her. He could no longer see her. He focused solely on the man. He wanted to rip the mask away to reveal the identity of this man while he burned like a dry stick over a campfire.

Yes, Sage wanted to burn him and revel in that burning. Fire was both life and death. Sage would use that power to exact justice, revenge, redemption.

He reached out his hand, pointing at the man's head. A fireball blew from Sage's extended fingers. The man squealed and leapt to the side, taking Marianne with him.

Marianne!

He mustn't hurt Marianne. But Sage was confident he could avoid hitting her.

The man gripped his fingers around her arms, eliciting a cry of pain while keeping her plastered against his chest. Sage's fury grew hotter and hotter until he enjoyed the feeling. He never quite understood the pleasure fury could bring to a man.

Until now…

He lifted his hand again. Another fireball shot from his fingertips. This time the man didn't have time to duck away. His arm caught fire. Marianne screamed as the man released her to slap at his arm. He managed to put out the fire and reclaim his hold on her, keeping her with him as he backed toward his tethered horse.

Sage would make certain the horse provided no aid. He moved his hand in the direction of the animal, preparing another fireball that would ensure the man had no escape left to him.

"No!"

He hesitated, sucking his breath in a harsh gasp. Marianne's voice crept into his brain, bringing reason...sanity.

No, not the horse. He'd never harm an animal. They were innocent creatures.

But he needed to allow no path for the man to escape. He looked again at the horse as it whinnied and reared, kicking at the surrounding trees.

Do no harm!

The horse deserved no harm, but the man was different. The man was evil. He held Marianne. *Held her against her will!*

Sage advanced. He lowered his head, staring at the man. A predator hunting prey.

A light appeared somewhere, illuminating the man with a bright glow so Sage could view every detail perfectly. The man's eyes were blue as he suspected. His brow was beaded with sweat, a drop of which ran down his temple until it touched the mask and disappeared. The cloth of his mask puffed in and out with rapid succession as the man fought for breath in his fright. His eyes were as round as goose eggs.

Sage smiled.

"Sage!" Marianne screamed. The sound of her fear should have angered him, but something in the way she spoke his name made him aware of her fear. Fear directed at him, not the highwayman. It shocked him.

His gaze strayed to her.

For the first time since he became free of his bonds, Sage looked at her. Truly looked at her.

Marianne's eyes were as round as the highwayman's, the fright in her face sickened Sage.

She feared him.

Why would Marianne fear Sage? He loved her. He would never harm her. She was like family. No, she was more than family...

He wished to protect her. Care for her. She was his responsibility. The first person he ever felt the need to take under his wing, the first person who ever needed his help.

She needed him and he needed her.

He would never hurt her.

So why did she look at him with such fear?

Sage stopped moving. He straightened, studying Marianne. Trying to understand why she was frightened.

"Sage," she said, her voice cracking. Her lips trembled as she spoke his name. Tears streamed down her cheeks. Sage felt a blow to his gut. He had made her cry.

"Marianne."

He spoke her name as an apology, as a plea for forgiveness. He never wanted to frighten her. The mere thought dashed the fire of anger with a splash of icy cold revulsion.

The flames licking at his hands, his body, his face shriveled and retreated back into his skin. Yes, his body had been consumed with flame. He hadn't noticed during his wrath. And now the warmth evaporated, leaving him cold and vulnerable. His hands shook. His knees trembled. His gaze fell to the ground as the realization of what occurred slapped his consciousness.

Sage clasped his shoulder as the pain returned with brute force. He fell to his knees.

Hurried footsteps pounded the road. Sage glimpsed the man abandon Marianne and run for his horse. He grabbed the animal, leapt into the saddle and galloped away.

Sage could have taken chase. He could have leapt to his feet and flung a fireball at the man's retreating back. With Marianne nowhere near him, he had no trepidation of missing his target.

Instead, Sage looked back at the ground.

He let the man go.

And he felt Marianne's gaze upon him. Sage could not bear to face her after what he'd just done. He had tried to kill the man. Sage had become the monster of his imagination.

The fire breathing dragon…a beast…a *demon*.

What was he?

The possibilities astounded him. The thoughts circling round his head terrified him, shocked him.

Was he truly a monster?

These last few moments confirmed it. He still felt the heat from the blaze at his back as the carriage continued to burn. The light flickered over him, casting eerie shadows on the road. He leaned forward, resting the palms of his hands on the ground, his fingers clenching, burying the dirt beneath his fingernails until spasms of pain shot through his hands.

He tried to ignore the sound of Marianne stepping closer. He wanted her to stop. To turn away. Run away. Far away from him and the beast living inside him.

Instead he closed his eyes and retched.

Chapter Six

Marianne's hands shook. Her whole body trembled as she watched Sage. She yearned to run to him, hold him in her arms, comfort him in some way. She wanted to reassure herself that he was unharmed. He certainly did not appear all right.

Something was wrong. Terribly, terribly wrong.

She had convinced herself the fire in the ballroom at Winfield had been a bizarre accident involving the misfortune of a close candle. He must have brushed against one without anyone having seen it.

Now, doubts resurfaced.

Sage had promised to speak with her about what Desmonda Green had told him. About the demon. Marianne couldn't help but wonder if this had something to do with what he wished to discuss.

Marianne watched him, waiting for some sign of what she must do. How could she help him? If only she knew, it might lessen the pain in her heart as she listened to him retch. After he finished, she heard his sobs. Quiet, soft whimpers in the night. He tried to suppress them, but they seemed to bubble up from deep within.

How long had he kept this secret?

Images flashed from moments ago, quickening the beating of her heart, the memories seared into her brain. She would never forget the terrible beauty of him as he advanced on his prey.

The fire had started gently, simmering from his skin, low soft flames caressing his neck and shoulders, rippling along his body until his entire being was swallowed in flame. The ropes burned away and the wheel caught fire. He stepped away from the remnants of the carriage with sensual movements that awed her.

Of course, as soon as she saw the flames, panic and fear consumed her. *Sage was on fire!* She cried out in horror and grief. *Her friend! Her dearest friend! He was on fire!* Her first thought was to run for water. Find a river, a lake, a stream, anything to douse him, to save him. *Save him!*

But there was nothing. They stood along an empty stretch of country road passing through a forested area of which she was completely unfamiliar. She had not the first clue where to find the water she so desperately needed to help her friend.

Grief struck her as she watched him burn.

And then he walked toward her. No, walking was not the correct word to describe what he had done. His head had lowered as he concentrated on the man holding her. The rage on his face something she had never witnessed on anyone, but especially never Sage.

His wrath surprised her. Marianne had seen him irritated before and annoyed, but never angered to such a passionate degree. Fury pulsed from within while flames licked his body, caressing his skin like a lover's touch.

Once he had the highwayman in his sights, he stalked toward him. Yes, that word suited his movements. Stalked, like a predator, with his head lowered, his gaze boring into the man with loathing hate.

Marianne recognized that Sage was protecting her. If the man hadn't been holding her as a shield, his response might have been of a different sort. But those actions sparked the fury within, igniting the flames as he hunted the highwayman, urging the man to release her and run. Running would provide a clear shot of killing him.

She knew Sage wanted to kill this man.

He shot those fireballs, aiming perfectly so she was not hit. Though, to be sure, she feared the man might jerk her into the fireball's path at the last critical moment. He used her as a shield after all.

But, no, it seemed Sage knew how the man would react and knew just what to do. The fireballs came at him, not to hit but to frighten him. Away from her. And then he would be an easy target to kill.

That's what she feared most…seeing the desire to kill in Sage's face.

What would that do to him, to his soul, if he killed this man? Would it mark him? Irreparably damaging his goodness, his heart? She could not allow him to do such. Sage needed to remain in the light.

Growing up, Marianne had heard stories of how easily witches turned from light to dark. And Sage would never desire to become a dark witch. She could not allow this momentary lapse in judgment to mar his soul for the rest of his life.

She screamed his name. The sound of her voice snapped him out of whatever control the rage had overcome. He looked at her for the first time instead of the man. She watched the fury release, draining from him. The expression in his eyes pierced her heart.

Surprise, grief, self-loathing. It all flashed over his face in a matter of moments. Marianne wanted to run to him then, as the flames subsided and he crumpled to the ground. She wanted to enfold him in her arms, embrace him in a protective sheath to keep him safe from all harm.

But she held herself still, afraid of how he might react to her touching him.

Touching him!

In those quick moments that seemed to last a lifetime, she'd forgotten about the odious powder the man had flung at her; the moment when another human being had touched her for the first time in close to a year. The ecstasy of the moment, the disbelief, the fear that it was merely a dream raced through her.

What had the man done to her? Was she no longer a spirit? Was that powder the cure they had been searching for? So many questions, and distantly she remembered the men had run off with the horses leaving her and Sage stranded.

Sage's sobbing slowed to a stop. He rested his forehead on the road, breathing heavily, his dirt-stained hands clutching the dark strands of his hair.

She took a deep breath, searching for a scrap of courage necessary to move her feet. She found the bravery she needed by looking at him.

Marianne knelt beside him. Her hand hovered over his back for several moments. She hesitated to touch him, not because he frightened her but because she was uncertain if her ability to touch vanished with that man. What if the powder did not cure her? What if it was a trick?

There was one way to be certain.

She rested her hand on Sage's back.

The warm sweat-soaked shirt covering the powerful muscles bunched beneath her fingertips. She moved her hand along his spine, feeling the ridges of bone, until she reached his neck as he slowly sat up. Her hand curved behind his neck, her fingers moving gently into his damp hair. Slowly, he turned. She looked into his eyes, finding wonder and disbelief.

Was this a dream?

Tears blurred her vision. Then suddenly her arms were around his neck, and she leaned her face into his hair, thrilled at the way the wet strands brushed against her cheek. His hands were on her back, clutching her dress, warm against her chilled skin.

They held each other for an eternity. And she felt it all. The warmth of his skin, his breath against her neck, his heart beating against her chest.

It felt so wonderful.

She cried. His hair soaked with her tears.

When they pulled apart, his cheeks were wet and his eyes bloodshot. She ran her fingers down his neck, along his shoulders and arms, touching him, enjoying the feel of him. Then her hand brushed against something wet and warm. She looked at the blood on her fingers.

"You're wounded?"

He simply nodded. She touched the buttons on his shirt, opening them one by one until she could push the fabric aside to expose the wound on his shoulder.

"It seems to have grazed you," she said after a quick inspection.

"And here," he said, sliding the shirt off completely. He pointed to his midsection. She leaned down to get a better view of his side.

"Grazed there, too. Bad shots," she said, smiling. "Lucky for you."

He grunted. She didn't think he agreed with the luck part. She reached for his shirt, about to help him put it back on when his hand on hers stopped her. He held it, his thumb sliding over her fingers.

"I'm very glad to have you back, Marianne," he said quietly.

She sucked in her breath and stared at him for a long moment. It struck her suddenly that she sat upon Sage's lap in the middle of nowhere with his shirt removed. His naked flesh gleamed in the moonlight. His broad chest stretched for miles; his nipples puckered as a gentle night breeze blew against them. Her gaze traveled to the corded muscles of his abdomen. Sleek, smooth skin over bumpy ridges. Her hand slid down his chest, touching his skin, caressing the tightened muscles beneath.

She heard his sharp intake of breath, then she yanked her hand away.

This was Sage! Why was she touching his body like this?

Heat flushed up her neck. Warmth grew in the deep pit of her belly. It never bothered her before that he was handsome and strong, with a body made like Adonis. But after touching him, she craved more…

Perhaps it was the spell. She seemed compelled to touch. With nearly a year without human contact, she *needed* to touch someone.

But this was Sage!

She scrambled off his lap, kneeling next to him instead. She cleared her throat before speaking, trying to adjust her thoughts appropriately.

"I apologize," she said at last. "That was inappropriate."

"I—"

"I'm not deluding myself, Sage," she said quickly, halting his response. She couldn't bear to hear what he had to say about her touching him so intimately. Better to avoid the subject. "This physical state may be temporary. When my spirit withdrew from my body, I saw my body afterward. I'm not certain how I can become whole again if my body is not near enough for my spirit to enter."

"Perhaps it doesn't work that way."

Marianne lifted one shoulder in a slight shrug. "True. But I'm not counting on it. Not until I can be certain."

"How can you be certain?"

"When I see my body is no longer where we left it, then I'll know."

"Magic works mysteriously, Marianne."

"I know. I've also thought about this often in the past year. These are some of the questions I dealt with while Drake had my body trapped in his castle."

"Drake." Sage said his brother's name like it was a foul word. He turned away, his lips twisting in a sneer.

Marianne leaned back to get a better view of Sage. Not his body, but the way he held himself. She arrived at a sensible conclusion.

"Drake was behind this, wasn't he?"

"What do you mean?"

"All of it," she said. "The highwaymen, the attack, the powder that man used, your new...fire magic." She said the last gently, considering at the last moment whether she should include it in her list. She wasn't certain if Drake had anything to do with that or not. It was a mere guess. Sage's hand catching fire at Winfield Park could be a coincidence, but she suspected it was part of whatever new magic Sage possessed.

These fire spells had the feel of a darker kind of magic than what he normally practiced. It was possible Sage could be practicing new spells, but he didn't seem the sort of witch that delved into anything classified as black magic. This magic was something Marianne knew Drake experimented with.

Sage's silence confirmed her suspicions.

"We should go," Marianne said. "You'll have to get those wounds cleaned and I…" She paused with a sigh. "I just want to go home."

"Of course," he said, and she helped him stand.

Chapter Seven

With limited magical abilities, their only option to get home was on foot. Sage knew spells that would transport them short distances, such as from one room to another in a house, and mirror spells which could send them longer distances, but at the moment, they weren't privy to a mirror.

They walked for hours with no inn or refuge in sight. The inn where he'd planned to stop was farther along this road, but at this pace, he feared they might not reach it until midday tomorrow. The pain of his wounds kept him at a rather slow gait.

Sage trudged wearily, noting the night grew darker as the moon traveled across the sky. Then clouds blew in from the east, masking any remaining light the moon shed. They were well and truly cast into darkness.

Marianne walked at his left where she continued her attempt to cast a light spell to no effect. Sage knew she found it highly disturbing to discover her new corporeal body possessed no magical abilities whatsoever. Before she'd been cursed, she had the natural abilities witches born with magic possess. Although like all witches, she needed to practice magic in order to become proficient. But casting a simple light spell to illuminate their path was one of the first spells even children used to light their nurseries at night when they woke to hear a strange noise.

If she couldn't cast simple spells such as that, what of the more complicated spells she had spent years studying and practicing?

"This is absurd," she mumbled after more than a dozen attempts.

"Perhaps you're trying too hard," Sage suggested. "After all, it's been a long time since you've cast any spells."

"Not this one," Marianne stated. "I've cast light spells all my life. It's like breathing."

This might be an overstatement, but Sage understood her meaning. This spell had come naturally to her and now...nothing.

"I'm done with this nonsense," Marianne said, with a deep sigh. "My fingers are getting sore from all the snapping. What of you? Why haven't you tried a light spell?"

Sage grimaced. He held out his hand like it didn't belong to him, as if it were someone else's hand. It didn't feel like it belonged. The magic from his fingertips was otherworldly.

"I don't think it's a good idea for me to make the attempt."

"Even a light spell?"

"I'm not certain if I can control it." He didn't admit that he was curious now. He hadn't tried such a simple spell in many months. Perhaps his ability to control whatever had become of his magic had strengthened. It seemed the fire magic emerged when he lost control of his emotions, when anger and fury overwhelmed him. But now he was calm. And he had managed to douse the flames with a mere look from Marianne. It could be she gave him the strength he needed to control the magic.

"It's a simple enough spell." He imagined a ball of light appearing above his hand. He focused on the image, concentrated on it until he the image was solid in his mind, then he spoke a few words and snapped his fingers.

Instead of the ball of white light appearing above his hand, five tiny flames shot out of his fingertips. They flickered for a moment before coming together to form one brighter flame hovering over the palm of his hand.

Marianne jumped, startled by the fire instead of a ball of light she was accustomed to seeing.

Sage stared with dismay at the flames, watching them dance over his hand. It was as he feared. Every spell he tried, every incantation he whispered was tainted by the demon's magic. He couldn't even perform a light spell without the fire interfering.

"Well," Marianne said. "It's not the light spell we normally cast, but it's bright enough to light our way."

Sage's lips lifted involuntarily upward. Leave it to Marianne to view the bright side of his dark ability.

"Look there," she said, pointing. "I see something."

He raised his hand in the direction she pointed, intensifying the fire so the light illuminated farther ahead. The outline of a man-made structure emerged from the inky blackness. At first he suspected it was the inn, perhaps nearer than he surmised, but as the light continued to shine from the growing flame he saw the structure was much smaller than an inn. It was a cottage, abandoned from the looks of the door hanging ajar, the overgrown foliage creeping up the walls and the hole in the thatched roof.

"Your…uh…your hand is on fire." Marianne's voice quavered.

Sage looked at his raised hand. Indeed, the flames curled around each finger, then down his palm and onto his wrist.

He turned his hand, wriggling his fingers as the flames danced in the darkness.

"Damn," he muttered. He couldn't control the flames to perform a light spell.

"Does it hurt?" Marianne asked softly.

"No," he said. "It surprises me each time. Perhaps it's merely instinct to react with fear at the sight of fire."

"Especially fire spouting from your fingertips."

"Exactly," he agreed. "It takes every ounce of self-control to not run screaming from myself."

"And it doesn't harm you in any way. There is no damage to your skin, not even your clothes," Marianne added, as she observed the fire bursting from his skin.

"None. It's part of the magic, I suppose."

"How do you do it?"

He had vowed not to speak of his fire magic to anyone. He'd been too horrified to admit what had happened. But he knew he must speak to someone. To have another witch hear of what occurred, so he wouldn't feel alone. But was he truly prepared to speak of how he obtained the magic? To Marianne? She was so young, so innocent. Could he cloud her mind with such dark images as the horrible deeds done to him at the hands of a demon?

He sickened at the thought. "Let's seek shelter, shall we?"

Avoidance would work well for tonight. He'd think

of a better way to avoid the explanation later. At the moment, he was too weary to speak.

Marianne did not move immediately. As he limped away, she remained behind. He felt her gaze on the back of his neck, but nothing she could do or say might compel him to tell her what had occurred that night in Blackmoor. In fact, the only other being who knew what had happened was the very demon that attacked him. Thanks to Marianne's sister, Julia, the demon was no longer able to touch him. She had killed it during their escape from Drake's castle.

"Very well," Marianne said after a moment. Relief sagged his shoulders to hear she planned not to pursue her need for answers. Knowing her most of his life, he knew that cost her great restraint.

Sage approached the cottage, aware this abandoned building might be the current residence for any number of wild creatures. He used the light from the fireball to illuminate the cottage, pushing the door open, expecting something to skitter from the corners of the cottage.

To his surprise, nothing stirred. The cottage might be abandoned, but it was not the complete disaster that he expected. The trestle table in the center of the room bore a thick layer of dust, as did the other items found in the house, but he could live with a bit of dirt. His major concern was finding a place in which to rest his weary head for the night.

Sage's eyelids had grown heavy, and his shoulder and knee hurt like the devil. He wanted nothing more than to sleep and wake refreshed in the morning, prepared to start a new day.

Marianne entered the cottage behind him, slowly taking in her new surroundings. While she perused their lodgings for the night, he found a bit of kindling and stashed it in the dusty hearth, lighting it with his hand.

As the fire caught hold of the kindling, Sage closed his eyes and concentrated on extinguishing the fire in his hand. When he opened them, he was dismayed to find the flames still burning brightly on his skin. He squatted beside the hearth.

"What's wrong?"

"I have trouble controlling it," he explained. "It won't extinguish."

"How did you do it before?"

"I don't know," he said, anger sparking heat to his words. If he knew what he did before, he'd do it again. It was a daft question.

Sage blinked, his frustration mounting. He shouldn't snap at her because of it.

He took a deep breath before he answered honestly.

"Before...I was embarrassed when I realized what I'd nearly done. I was horrified you witnessed it." He wouldn't voice the thoughts of killing the man, although he was certain she knew.

"Well, I wouldn't wish for you to feel that way every moment you used magic such as this."

"I bloody well am horrified," he growled. "This is the only magic I have left."

"What do you mean?"

"Every spell I attempt goes uncontrollably wrong." Sage turned to Marianne as she walked forward to inspect his hand. "Casting spells a child might use and yet this fire appears."

Marianne's eyes widened the slightest bit. She looked away, hoping he wouldn't notice her trepidation, but he did.

"This must be a temporary condition," she suggested. Her gaze reconnected with his. Anything else she planned to say died away.

"It's been long enough. I don't think it's temporary."

She had nothing else to offer. Instead, she frowned and looked again at the flames. Her expression changed. Something new flickered in her gaze, an unspoken query. Slowly, she raised her arm, reaching out to his hand, cupping her fingers against the heat on his palm.

"What are you doing?" He drew back. Did she wish to burn? The flames did no damage to his skin, but he was enchanted. Marianne had no protection against the fire.

"No, don't," she whispered. He hesitated, wondering what she meant to do.

At first he thought he imagined the chill as she neared. The flames danced and flickered when her hand grew closer, then orange and yellow wavered. Slowly, she lowered her hand closer to his, watching in equal amazement as the flames grew smaller and shorter. When at last, her fingers grasped his palm, a shiver rippled along his arms. The flames died away leaving nothing between his hand and hers.

Her hand was like ice.

Cold.

Like death.

"Marianne?"

The rest of his question went unspoken when she looked up, tearing her gaze away from his hand to stare into his eyes.

"I'm chilled. My body hasn't warmed at all. I

thought I might grow warm as the night wore on, but it hasn't happened yet."

"Perhaps by morning?"

"I'm not weary either. As a spirit, my energy did not weaken day or night. There was no reason to rest nor sleep. I assumed once I regained my body I would grow tired again. But even after all of this walking tonight, I'm not weary at all. I feel the same as I have all evening."

"But I can *feel* you." Sage emphasized the point by squeezing her hand. Warmth blossomed in his chest at the contact even cold as it was to touch. "This is your body. You are back with us."

Marianne shook her head. The sadness on her face wrenched his heart. After all of this time existing in spirit form, she did not believe her good fortune.

"Julia and Father had lived at Blackmoor for some time. Do you recall?"

"Yes, that's when you came to live at Merriweather Manor."

Marianne nodded. "Father had promised Drake that he would help him search for a cure for Susanna. She was so sick. Drake would do anything to save his wife. Father helped him in his laboratory while Julia tended to Susanna. After she died, Drake went mad. He and Father had been working on a potion that would keep Susanna's body alive, even after her spirit departed. He said it would give him more time to find a cure. But Father stopped him from administering the potion at the last moment. He said the magic was dark, and it would blacken his soul, not to mention the horror Susanna's spirit might suffer…A ghost in limbo, unable to step into the ever-after, to rejoin our ancestors."

Marianne paused, biting her lip.

Sage reached for her hand, squeezing it.

"Drake vowed revenge. Not long after, Father died mysteriously. We have no proof, but Julia is convinced Drake killed him."

Sage's brother…a murderer. It didn't sit well. His brother had gone to university to learn medicine to help people, not hurt them. But after the madness took him, who was to say how that altered his mind?

"I did not believe it. Not Drake. So last summer, I visited Blackmoor. I merely wished to ease Julia's grief that our father was not murdered." Marianne's voice softened, as she gazed into the fireplace. Sage wondered if she saw the past in those flames.

"We drank tea," she said. "It was spicy, but delicious. I asked for more. Drake obliged, happily. We chatted. I faltered at approaching the subject of Susanna and my father. Before I gathered enough courage to speak, my stomach pained me. Awful spasms of pain. I dropped the tea, splashing it on his carpet. I remember wanting to apologize for that…"

Her voice trailed off. She was trapped there, in that room with his brother, drinking and enjoying the very tea that contained the potion that Drake used to curse her. Sage had heard a shortened version of this story before, from Julia and Basil.

He never spoke of it to Marianne. She had never been forthcoming with talk of the night Drake cursed her. If he referred to it, she'd nod and carry on with the conversation, never embellishing the details of that night as she was now.

"When I woke, I lay crumpled on the floor of his parlor. I was alone. I didn't realized what had occurred until I reached for the handle of the door. My hand passed through the wood."

"Marianne…" The pain in her voice tugged at his heart. He could not imagine the horror she had suffered when she realized what Drake had done.

"He sent word to Julia. She arrived a day later. I'll never forget the look on her face when she saw my body on that bed. I could have killed Drake myself for what he did to my sister. The grief she suffered, losing Father and then me. He blackmailed her, promising that if she helped him find the spell to bring back his wife's spirit into another body, he'd release me. He'd give her the spell that would save me. She had no choice but to agree.

"Of course, Basil returned, ruining her chances for bargaining with Drake. But it turned out well enough in the end. You found my body, returned it to Merriweather Manor. And now here I am…" She lifted her arms, looking at her hands. "I have a body again. But…it does not feel the same, Sage. Something is wrong. I know it."

"Marianne." He leaned forward, pulling her closer. Now that the fire was gone from his hand, he felt no compunction in embracing her. He wrapped his arms around her, holding her chilled body. Her fingers curled around the lapel of his shirt. "We'll get through this. I promise you."

Her head tilted up until her face was a mere breath away from his own. She stared into his eyes, and he felt as if she searched his soul. Not certain what she searched for, he returned her gaze until he noticed something else in her eyes. Something he glimpsed on the road earlier this night.

Suddenly he was aware of every part of her body touching his. Every curve brushed against him in a way he never recalled.

Marianne was a dear friend, but in this moment she was something much, much more.

Sage's breath caught when he recognized the sudden heat in her eyes. Her gaze flickered innocently to his lips. His heart pounded at the sight of her mouth opening just the barest bit, as if she thought to speak but failed to find the words.

He brushed his lips against her mouth. At first, he hadn't realized he'd moved. His head bent toward her as if drawn by some unknown power.

He kissed her, and it felt right to do so.

Marianne's hand slid from his lapel to his shoulder, where she gripped him tightly. Her fingers clenched onto his wound sending agony ripping through him until he broke apart from the kiss with a groan of pain.

"Oh!" Marianne jumped. "I'm sorry! I did not mean to… I did not realize…"

"It's quite all right, Marianne." Sage attempted a reassuring smile. It felt more like a grimace.

"It's not. Here, let us see the damage. I hope I didn't make it worse." She tugged at his shirt to expose the wound to view. He looked away. Anger and embarrassment warred within him.

Had he just kissed Marianne? More importantly…had she responded in kind?

Marianne's gasp drew him away from his thoughts.

"What?" He prepared for grim news. It was too early to tell if infection had set in, but he was also aware if he did not clean and bandage it soon, chances of infection were great.

"It's healing."

The wonder and disbelief in her voice drew his attention more than her actual words. He looked at his shoulder. The bleeding had stopped, leaving reddish brown streaks dried on his skin, but the wound itself appeared smaller than it had previously.

"Are you certain?"

"Indeed, I am. Do you note the edges? They've mended. The wound was far larger than this."

He agreed.

"How does it feel? Does it hurt?"

"Like the devil," he said. It was true. His shoulder ached and throbbed, the pain only lessening a degree if he remained incredibly still.

"Did you use some spell to mend it?"

"No. I cannot. If I attempt any spell, the fire…"

"Yes," Marianne said, nodding. "Well, in any case, it seems to be healing. We'll keep a watch on it."

Sage agreed, then sat back. He raised his arms to the fire burning in the hearth, welcoming the warmth that soon filled the room.

The memory of their kiss filled Sage's mind. He didn't look at Marianne for fear of the loathing he might see in her eyes. He was like a brother to her. What must she be thinking of him? What had possessed him to kiss her, even something as light as brushing their lips together? Did it qualify as a kiss? In fact, he'd never experienced such an innocent encounter as that brief contact.

As he pondered the kiss and how to explain it to Marianne, his eyelids grew heavy. Soon, his head started tilting forward.

Marianne's cold fingers gently guided his head

down onto her lap. He rested on the cottage floor and slept.

****

As Marianne watched him sleep, she thought of their shared kiss.

With one hand, she carefully brushed her fingers through his short, dark hair, enjoying the feel of the silky strands against her skin. The other hand she used to touch her lips, trying to imitate the feel of him caressing her.

Chills coursed through her at the memory.

Stuff and nonsense. It must be. He was only being kind, trying to comfort her when she was so uncertain of her future.

A friendly kiss, nothing more. Men and women shared friendly kisses, did they not?

Truly, Marianne did not know. She never had close friends other than the Merriweathers, and thoughts of kissing them had never struck her mind. The men were much older than her own twenty years. Sage was in fact the youngest Merriweather male, and he was not more than six years her senior. Most of the girls were closer to her own age, Lillian, Melora and Senna. Hyacinth was older but still close enough that they all had great fun as children.

She couldn't ask for better friends than the Merriweathers. Having any of them, even Sage who was in her mind the most handsome, as anything more than simple friends was inconceivable.

After all, she had David to think about.

David!

With all the excitement with the carriage, the highwaymen and then her regaining her body, she had all but forgotten what it might mean for her.

Now she could marry David.

She looked at the sleeping Sage, and a curious emotion stirred within her chest. What was it?

It was odd, whatever it might be.

And strangely, she did not wish to think of David. Instead, she was content to sit on the dusty floor of the abandoned cottage, holding Sage's head in her lap and watch him sleep.

After a few hours of sitting in the same position, Marianne's stomach began to feel strange. Queasy. She had never felt such a queer sensation.

With gentle care, she removed Sage's head from her lap, lowering him onto the floor. Quietly, she stood. The world wobbled for a bit. When it righted itself again, she searched for a chair to sit upon. A dusty one sat in the corner, but she, with no care for dirt, sat.

The queasiness subsided.

Strange. Since she couldn't understand why she'd be struck with such stomach disturbance, she sat for a bit longer for fear it might return. After staying still several long minutes, noticing the symptoms did not return, she began to rest easy.

Her attention returned to Sage snoring softly on the floor. He looked so young while he slept. Like an innocent boy instead of the rakish man he had become. Since she was so much younger, she had never known Sage when he was a small child, so she couldn't compare his features now to the lad of his youth. In her imagination, he looked as he did now.

Dark eyelashes swept over his pale cheeks. The skin around his eyes and brow were softened from the tension she recently noticed stretched there at all times.

And his mouth curved into a lax smile of contentment, again something she had not seen in quite a while.

A noise from outside tore her attention from her sleeping companion. Marianne's breath stilled in her chest as she strained to listen.

There it was again.

The crunch of footsteps, like someone walking outside the cottage. She glanced at the windows which were shuttered tight against the outside elements. Not knowing how secure they were made her uneasy.

Who might be wandering the country at this time of night? Could those highwaymen have returned to exact revenge?

She glanced at Sage, but decided not to wake him. Yet. Perhaps it was merely the wind blowing branches against the house or her wild imagination conjuring assumptions out of nothing. Whatever it might be, she did not wish to wake Sage until she knew for certain if any danger was present. In his weakened state, he needed sleep to recover from his ordeal.

Marianne stood and crept closer to the door. Not thinking they might be approached by ruffians during the night, they hadn't latched it when they entered the cottage. Their thoughts had been elsewhere.

She pulled open the door, wincing at the soft groan of rusted hinges. When she had enough space to peer out, she searched the inky darkness for any sign of movement. Nothing alerted her.

Again she strained to listen for any noise to indicate someone outside, but she heard none.

Not assured of their safety, Marianne took a bold step out of the cottage, preparing a scream to awaken Sage at the first sign of any movement. Again, she wondered if it had been her imagination.

Just to be certain, she walked into the darkness to search around the cottage.

Chapter Eight

He dreamed of that night.

In all his days, nothing had prepared Sage for the night he met a demon in his brother's castle.

It had been impulsiveness on Basil's part, throwing himself into the mirror when Julia disappeared. Neither Basil nor Sage knew where the mirror had transported her, but it did not matter. The fact that Julia Grey faced danger was enough for Basil to go after her, with every intention of rescuing her.

As soon as Basil vanished into the mirror, the glass wavered and flexed, like water in a pond that had been disturbed.

Sage had seconds to decide what must be done. He could go for help, but what good would it do for Basil and Julia if he knew not where they were? The mirror passage could take them anywhere another mirror stood. Granted, mirrors were not a common item in every household in all the world, but enough so to make it impossible to perform a thorough search. Once the portal closed, he might never find them again.

Only one option remained.

He turned to Marianne. Her face was one of shock as she stared at the mirror that had just consumed her sister.

"Stay here." His voice snapped her attention to him.

"Sage!" The alarm in her voice matched the horror blossoming on her face. He tried not to allow her fear to sway him to reconsider. His brother and her sister were in danger. He must help.

"You will stay and await our return, do you understand?" Sage told her in the only authoritative voice he could muster, not one he often had occasion to use. But he had to be certain she would not follow. He had enough worry with Basil and Julia. When she didn't respond, simply stared at him, he repeated loudly, "Understand?"

"Y-yes," Marianne said, nodding her head violently.

She was shaking. For a moment Sage wished to comfort her, reassure her that all would be well, and he would return with her sister, but he could promise no such thing. Since he could not touch her anyway, the urge was moot.

Without another word, Sage stepped into the mirror.

The liquid glass wrapped around him like a cloak. He instinctively held his breath, though he knew from prior experience his lungs would still function. As soon as the glass slid along his back, fully consuming him, the disorientation began in full. His body stretched across great distances and in doing so he felt pulled apart. His arms yanked from his shoulders, his legs were dragged behind. Although it was a peculiar and slightly uncomfortable sensation, it did not hurt. It felt as if a great time had lapsed, but it was mere seconds later when he stumbled through the opposite mirror, arriving at his destination in one piece and unharmed.

Stone floor connected with his booted feet. He

stumbled but managed to stay upright. Barely.

This was one of many reasons witches didn't commonly use mirror travel. The arrival was always an ordeal. He knew witches who had broken arms by arriving, then stumbling on their feet to smack into walls or other furniture. It was a less than graceful mode of transportation, though in a pinch it would do.

Basil lay crumbled on the floor. His brother Drake stood over him.

Sage blinked, not certain he saw clearly.

"Drake, old boy," Sage said, confused. "What are you doing here?"

Marianne had said Julia had contacted a necromancer who was blackmailing her into stealing the Merriweather grimoires. She said nothing about Drake Merriweather helping her.

"Ah, Sage," Drake said. "So glad you've joined us."

A spell flew from Drake's lips. A moment later, Sage was unable to move. He tried to force his limbs, pushing at the invisible barrier that pinned him. It did no good. He was bound in spell.

"This was not part of our bargain," Julia said.

Julia was here.

Sage could hear everything, but he could only see what came into his view. From one corner of his vision, Julia stooped to assist Basil to his feet.

"Drake," Basil said, as he stood. "What have you done?"

"No time for a reunion, dear brother. We've work to do, haven't we, Julia?" And with another quickly worded spell, Drake bound Basil.

"No, Drake, release them. Send them back. You

have what you need. They can do you no harm. Send them back!" Julia's outraged voice met his ears as she moved away from his line of sight.

"You will help me find the correct formula," Drake said, his voice a raspy growl more like an animal than a man. "After we've found the spell, I will honor our agreement."

"Truly?" Doubt colored her voice.

"I may have gone mad, Julia, but I still honor my promises."

Sage had difficulty following any conversation after that. Drake led Julia from the room. Within moments, he returned and undid the spell confining Sage.

Sage's legs wobbled, and he sank to the floor.

"Sage," Drake said, then squatted next to him. "It saddens me to see you here, brother."

"Well, I had to go after them," he explained. "I didn't know you were here. Basil just threw himself into the mirror to chase after Julia. I couldn't let him go alone."

"Of course not," Drake said, a small smile lifting the corners of his mouth though it never reached his eyes. Drake had sad eyes. In fact, a smile hadn't touched his brother's eyes since Susanna died. Drake's wife had meant the world to him. Her death came at great cost to his brother's happiness.

"Drake, what *are* you doing here?" Sage's mind began to create an abundance of possibilities for his brother's presence. Some of those possibilities were far more disturbing than he cared to admit.

But Drake ignored his query.

"Always the hero, Sage. Always the one to ride to

the rescue when anyone needs you. You were there for me, too, brother, when Basil was not. He found other things more important than family. When I was in great pain, he needed to fulfill his wanderlust. You tried to help me, but I pushed you away. Now, I think it's better if you go home."

"What's happening, Drake? Why are you here?"

"I live here, brother. You are in my home."

He stepped back so Sage had a better view. The stone walls revealed a room Sage had seen once before during one of his many visits to his brother's castle. Castle Blackmoor was a crumbling bit of real estate, but Drake had been proud to call it home. Susanna had loved it, too, which made it all the more precious to his brother.

This was Drake's laboratory. He was an inventor and a self-proclaimed scientist as well as a witch. After spending years at university, studying medicine and other sciences, he had come home and set up this room to assist in his experiments. He had made several advances before Susanna fell ill.

"Drake," Sage said his brother's name. A sour taste had formed on his tongue. "You..."

"Go home, Sage, please," Drake warned. "Before it's too late."

"What have you done to Basil? Where is Julia?"

Drake closed his eyes and sighed. "Always the hero."

Then he spoke quickly, casting the spell before Sage could repel it in defense.

Darkness swelled within Sage's eyesight, welcoming him unwillingly to sleep.

****

A soft feathery touch brushed against his cheek awakening Sage. He blinked several times, his eyelids feeling strangely glued together.

A raven-haired woman stood before him, a feather in one hand and a knowing smile on her face. She was beautiful. Her arched brows and thick black eyelashes framed dark brown eyes which focused on him. Red lips curved upward, revealing pearly white teeth. Her skin was flawless, like creamy silk.

The way she smiled, like she wished to devour him, intrigued him, and he found himself smiling in return.

Until he felt the chains binding his wrists.

"What the bloody hell?" Sage muttered, pulling against the chains only to find he was bound to a short leash that limited his movement. He couldn't even cross his arms. The chain was strapped to the wall behind him, and though he sat on the floor, he had little room to maneuver.

"You're awake. Good," the woman said. "Finally, I get to play."

"Who are you?" He glanced around the tiny room. It was sparse, with a desk and a chair. "Where are my brothers?"

"So many questions. All will be answered in time."

Then she leaned forward, closing the small gap between them. Her warm breath caressed his face. Her tongue plunged into his mouth, searching, caressing, kissing deeply. He wanted out of these chains, especially if a beautiful woman was willing to kiss him like this. He strained against the chains, trying to wrap his arms around her as well as gain his freedom. Sadly, he could do neither. Although, he'd never been averse to a bit of bondage in the bedroom.

When she finished kissing him, she drew back, licking her lips. Sage might have enjoyed such behavior at another time, in another place, but at this moment, it disturbed him that she regarded him as if he were some manner of prey.

Normally, he enjoyed spending time with bold women, yet something about this one sent signals of alarm racing through his skull.

"I've never been kissed by a woman I've not properly been introduced to."

She shook her head, slightly. "No need to know my name to enjoy the comforts and pleasures I'm willing to bestow unto you."

"Call me old-fashioned," he remarked. It made him considerably uneasy that she could not part with something as simple as her name.

The hairs on the back of his neck began to stand on end.

There was something in this room, something magical that differed from the sort he was used to sensing. It felt off somehow. If he could compare it to a piece of beef that had sat too long in the sun, he might say the magic felt rotten. As if it had gone sour. He couldn't quite understand. It made him uneasy, to say the least. The urge to run consumed him, threatening him with the notion that he was in great danger.

But this was Drake's castle. No harm had ever come to him here.

Sage tried to brush his uneasiness aside, but it remained, stubbornly so.

The woman dipped her head again, this time placing her warm lips on his cheek, kissing her way to his ear, where her lips and tongue wrapped around the lobe. His heart hammered loudly in his chest, not in sensual excitement, but in sudden fear.

Who was this woman? Why was she touching him in this way?

A day ago he might not have questioned her motives. What hot-blooded male would question good fortune such as this?

But with the momentous revelations he had discovered at home, what with Marianne's spirit being torn apart from her body, he couldn't help but feel this woman was connected in some way. As if she were an obstacle in his path. A beautiful, stunning obstacle, but an obstacle nonetheless.

"As much as I adore the attention you lavish upon me, I fear now is not an ideal time, my dear."

The woman leaned back until she looked into his eyes again.

"I have friends who need my help. I need to get out of these chains and find them. Would you mind?" Sage lifted his wrists in hopes she might free him.

The woman smiled again, seductively, and he thought for a moment he heard a growl emitting from her throat but assumed it must be a purring sound. Perhaps she imagined the sound might entice him.

Then she lunged at him, her mouth latching onto his throat, her teeth clamping on his skin, her tongue licking and tasting. Her hands roamed the rest of his body, caressing his arms, his chest, the back of his neck, running her fingers through his hair.

He closed his eyes and groaned.

This must be a dream. Some sort of erotic dream. It was the only explanation. Drake had cast a sleeping spell over him, and he still slumbered, prisoner to its seduction.

He shouldn't fight its pull. He shouldn't fight her. Who would want to stop this incredible experience?

But doubt lingered in his mind. This felt too real to be a dream. And the feeling of magic, that rotting magic, sickened him.

"Stop this." It sounded weak to his own ears. She wouldn't believe he wished for her to stop. But he needed to get out of here. Basil might be in danger. What was Drake doing? How had they ended up at Drake's castle when Marianne said Julia bargained with a necromancer?

There were too many questions that needed answering, and this woman was a barrier between him and the answers. She must go.

"Stop this!" He said the words again, this time with more force. "I have to get to my friends. They need my help."

She moved her mouth away from his neck. He met her gaze. The woman's eyes flashed red, flames appearing where her irises should be.

"No one can help them now," she said, smiling.

The evil in her face struck him. Suddenly he knew where the rotten magic was coming from.

The woman.

She reeked of it, this dark magic leaving his skin feeling sullied and dirty.

He lifted his right hand, spoke the words for a spell to push her away, a force to knock her back. He cast the spell, and she flinched from the magic. Then she lifted her head and smiled.

The spell did nothing but make her blink. He tried

it again, and again. Then he tried something more powerful, the force of twenty men attacking, and yet she barely flinched. Instead, she grew stronger, happier, more at ease with the violence he flung at her.

Her fingernails grew and lengthened, like the claws of an animal. She scratched his chest; a long vibrant line of red appeared. Then she laughed at his cries of pain.

He cast more spells, but he was feeling fatigued. All the energy and stamina he possessed drained. Soon when he cast spells nothing emerged. He felt his magic fading. It was as if every spell he cast was absorbed within her, and his magic went with it.

She began speaking to him then, telling him of what she planned to do to him. That he had been promised to her.

"Do you not like me?" she said, when she noticed her words did not sway him. "I picked this form to please you, but perhaps you like something else?"

Her face shifted, her skin vibrating in a quick fluid ripples until he stared at Marianne.

Marianne?

Yes, she had mutated into Marianne. He watched in horror as she approached him.

"Oh, gods!" he cried out. What was she that she could shift forms? He looked away.

What was she?

"Oh, you do like her! I knew you would," the creature crowed happily.

It was not Marianne's voice. The creature. That's how he must think of her since what human could mutate forms? What entity used such dark magic?

A demon.

She was a demon.

"But I do not like this body," she said. "Too skinny, by far. How is this?"

She pulled his hair, turning him to her, yanking his head back until his eyes opened to find Julia grinning at him. Julia's face with glowing, fiery eyes.

"This female has curves and a beautiful body." She leaned back and grabbed her breasts, caressing them, kneading them. "Alas, you do not find her attractive. Perhaps you'd enjoy this?"

It shifted again, and he saw his brother, Drake.

"Oh, gods!" Sage shouted, struggling, kicking his legs, swinging his feet. But the creature's strength proved too much for him.

"Ah, Sage," it said mimicking his brother's voice. "Do not give up on me. I enjoy your struggles."

But Sage's mind was being torn asunder. He could not think. He could not see. His mind was elsewhere, searching for something, anything to take him away from the torment she inflicted on his brain.

The creature had shifted again, this time back into her original form. And then her hair grew aflame, her neck and down to her breasts and then her arms. Her entire body consumed by fire. He screamed as the heat flashed over his body.

Then she sat on his lap.

Flames licked at his skin. He screamed, closing his eyes since he could not bear to watch himself burn. It soon sank into his brain that the fire did not damage him. It stung, it hurt, but as he burned with her, the flames merely covered his skin like a cloak. The intense heat was almost more than he could bear, yet it did not burn as he expected.

She laughed.

His body burned. Even his blood felt on fire. Every vein lit under his skin; with every heartbeat, it surged through him, into his arms and legs, into his body.

Her claw-like hands wrapped around his arms, the fire burning more intensely there. Her nails pierced his skin.

Sage knew he was going to die.

Chapter Nine

Marianne circled the cottage twice before deciding to step further into the darkened forest. She walked several steps away before crouching beside a large tree. There she stayed, listening, watching, patiently waiting for another suspicious sound to draw her attention. Although she found no sign of any human presence, she still felt that someone was in the forest, waiting, perhaps even watching her. She tried to cast another spell, something to help her locate any life larger than that of a rabbit or squirrel who might have found a home in the shrubs or trees surrounding her. But, her magic failed her. She frowned as she looked at her hands.

Why did her magic not work?

Another wave of nausea hit Marianne. She stood and leaned against the tree, gripping the bark beneath her fingernails. She waited for the wave to pass. It was sharper this time. Painful. Her stomach cramped, and she squeezed her eyes shut until it passed.

She took several deep breaths before she lifted her head.

What was that?

She sniffed the air trying to identify the odor. It smelled like smoke. But where…?

Marianne looked cautiously over her shoulder. It took a moment for her to comprehend the orange and red glow flickering through the trees.

Fire!

The cottage was on fire.

Sage!

She leapt to her feet, lifted her skirts and ran swiftly back to the cottage, hoping it was mere illusion. As she grew near, she saw it was not. Flames licked at the thatched roof, crawling up the walls.

"Sage!" she screamed, spinning in a circle, searching for any sign of him by the side of the road, staring in disbelief at what had become of their refuge. She saw no one.

Marianne turned back to the cottage, a horrified notion forming in her mind. What if he was still inside?

With her heart thudding, she hurried into the burning building. It felt much like walking into a lit oven. The fire consumed one half of the cottage, the walls and roof rippled with waves of flame. It would not be long before the entire structure would burn to the ground.

Sage lay on the floor where she left him. Sleeping? Or dead? She looked closer and gasped. *He was on fire!*

"Sage!" She screamed his name, going as close to him as she dared. The heat was overwhelming. The smoke clouded the air until she choked on it. She dropped to her hands and knees, crawling toward Sage and screaming his name over and over.

The heat became unbearable. Her chest grew tight with need for air. Her eyes squeezed shut, tears creeping out the sides as she coughed from the smoke.

She couldn't see him anymore.

"Sage!" She choked out once more, thrusting her hands out, searching blindly for him. Whether he was on fire or not, she had to find him.

Her fingers scraped the dirt floor which had grown warm from the heat. Nothing! Where was he?

Was he dead? Is that why he couldn't hear her? It was all her fault. She never should have left him. And now she would die with him. She tried searching again, but the fire surrounded her. She couldn't see anything but orange flame.

Strong hands gripped her waist. She was pulled from the floor and dragged away. She clung to the arms holding her and tried to move her feet. They were moving. But where? There was nowhere to hide in the flame.

"Close your eyes!"

With his arms wrapped tightly around her, she felt the vibrations of his roar while pressed against his chest. She quickly obeyed. He lifted her neatly into his arms, scooping her legs out from beneath her. A moment later, there was a crash. She felt his body impact the door, shaking her violently. Then a rush of cool air hit her face. She took several deep breaths, choking on the fresh air.

When she opened her eyes, she found herself lying on the edge of the road, looking up at the flames engulfing the cottage. It burned brightly, lifting ashes high into the sky.

Sage lay beside her, his face turned away. He was no longer burning, but the sight of him engulfed in flames had been seared upon her brain. She couldn't rid her mind of the horrifying image.

When she breathed easier, she placed her hand on his arm.

He rubbed his eyes with one hand, not looking at

her immediately. When he did, she saw the redness and knew he cried.

"Are you all right?" Her bottom lip trembled. "I thought you were dead." She tried to say more, but her voice cracked.

"Shh," Sage said, wrapping one arm around her. He drew her to him and held her while she buried her face against his chest. His warm chest. He was alive!

Marianne closed her eyes, gripping the cloth of his shirt in her hands as she held him, relishing the feel of him. *Alive!*

"I was dreaming…"

She lifted her head. A stricken look passed over his features. He seemed to gaze into nothingness.

"I was dreaming about…when it happened," he said, faltering for words. "It was…a nightmare. A nightmare. And then I heard you screaming my name. I woke, and I was on fire. Just like in my dream."

"Oh, Sage," Marianne said, putting one finger on his chin to draw his attention away from the fire or the nightmare he was currently reliving. He moved with her finger, his attention jumping from the fire to her face. His eyes widened, and she felt his chest shudder on a quick breath.

Suddenly, she realized how intimately they held each other. He cradled her in his arms, her body lying against his. She looked at his face, his eyes, his lips. She felt his warm breath. If she leaned in only a few inches, she could kiss him.

Was she so bold? Could she kiss him?

What would he say? Or do?

Would he kiss her back or push her away?

Fear and uncertainty gripped her. This was

Sage…her friend. He was like a brother. Was he not?

Then why did her heart pound rapidly in her chest, while every inch of her skin that contacted his throbbed with pleasure? His body was solid, where hers was soft. The difference between them shocked her, making her realize she'd never felt a man's body pressed against hers like this. He held her closer than any dance partner ever dared.

And she wondered if he might kiss her again. But how to explain that she yearned for more than a simple caress. She breathed heavily, nearly gasping for air. Was it the near death she had just confronted?

Whatever it may be, she wanted to kiss him. For a moment, she thought he meant to kiss her, too. His face hovered over hers, their lips drawing close together until…

Sage hesitated, an unspoken question in his eyes. Sense seemed to awaken him. He drew back. Marianne caught a brief glimpse of horror dawning on his countenance before he turned away.

Marianne felt ill. Nausea rippled through her as she realized what she had almost done, what he must think of her to see the desire in her eyes. She horrified herself. What a senseless fool!

How could Sage ever think of her as more than a sister? And why would she want him when she had David?

"It…" Marianne hesitated until she could focus on controlling her voice so it did not waver. She licked her lips. "At Winfield…It wasn't an errant candle that started the blaze, was it?"

"No."

****

The next day found Sage and Marianne walking along the country road yet again. When Marianne finally reached home, she vowed to never walk farther than she needed ever again.

After walking in silence for nearly an hour, Marianne heard the sound of a horse and wagon. A farmer approached from behind pulling a wagon of hay.

"Sage," she said to get his attention. "I believe salvation has come upon us."

He squinted into the sunlight. They awaited the farmer's approach. When he was within earshot Sage sent his greetings.

"Good day to you," he said, with a friendly wave. Marianne hoped the farmer did not inspect their attire too closely. A woman dressed in a frilly frock better suited to an evening of dancing than a day of walking the road and a man wearing a singed evening jacket might draw comment from the locals.

"Hello!" The farmer called back with a tip of his hat. "A fine day to be walking home from a ball."

Well, he had better eyesight than she hoped.

"Yes," Sage said, with a nonchalant shrug of his uninjured shoulder. "I hoped you might have room aboard your wagon for two passengers. I can offer you coin for your troubles."

"Keep yer coin, lad," the farmer said. "From the looks of it, you'll be needing it to get a new wardrobe."

Again Sage shrugged, a flush of embarrassment coloring his neck.

"Climb aboard. I'll take you to the end of the road. There's an inn yonder that will see to your needs. Where is your friend that we might hurry along?"

"Well…" Sage waved his hand in her direction.

"Wait," Marianne interrupted. Watching the farmer warily, she stepped in his direction to catch his attention. "Hello, there! Do you not see me?" She waved, a bright smile on her face so if he did see her, she might not appear that she belonged in Bedlam.

The farmer continued staring curiously at Sage, most likely due to Sage's hesitation in answering his most recent question. He did not glance in her direction, nor did he say any word in answer to her query. He simply waited in growing silence.

Marianne stepped toward the wagon. She reached out to touch the wooden slats. Instead of touching them, her fingers fell through.

Her spirits sank. She had expected this might occur. Her stomach clenched, and tears sprouted from the corners of her eyes.

"Marianne," Sage whispered.

But she couldn't acknowledge him. He believed whatever substance contained in that powder had cured her. But it was nothing more than a dream.

"What was that?" the elderly farmer asked, leaning forward with his hand to his ear to better hear Sage's whisper.

"My apologies," Sage said, as he climbed aboard the wagon. "Perhaps my friend will find another way home."

"Come along, Marianne," he whispered. "We'll sort this out."

She had little choice but to follow. She sat upon the edge of the wagon, her feet dangling over the back. A moment later the horses continued their slow journey. Sage sat next to her, silent while they gazed upon the road behind.

Chapter Ten

Instead of traveling to London as planned, Sage turned toward the country. Arriving at Merriweather Manor was usually an occasion for laughter and happiness. His childhood home was a warm place, full of love and friendship. Now that Basil, the eldest of the Merriweather siblings had arrived from years of traveling abroad, the sight of their home still brought a smile to his sad face.

Merriweather Manor provided comfort. This was the home of his brothers, sisters and his great-aunt Petunia, the matriarch of the family, as well as the home of his ancestors. Prior generations were born, lived and died here. Once the Merriweathers learned to stay hidden within society, to keep their powers from notice of non-magic-wielding humans, they had the opportunity to settle in one place instead of the constant roaming done by previous generations. The witch hunts had unsettled witches all over Europe. The terrible, dark times continued their fear of persecution, prompting them to keep their powers hidden from everyone save the magic-folk.

Returning home was something Sage did whenever he needed to seek shelter, comfort and the loving embrace of his family. It made sense to go there instead of his lonely town house in London during this time of…distress.

He wanted a hot bath and a soft bed. Sleeping on the floor of the cottage did not compare to the bed he was accustomed to.

In his room, the servants poured steaming buckets into his bath, then left. He leaned back against the warmed brass, allowing the heat of the water to soak into his weary bones. The stiffness he suffered since waking began to fade.

The door behind him opened.

"Go away," Sage said, without waiting to identify his unwanted visitor.

"I heard you were attacked on the road," Basil said.

Sage sighed. "News travels fast."

"Having been spotted walking up the drive instead of riding a horse was a good indication something out of the ordinary had occurred," Basil admitted. He leaned against the door frame, folding his arms across his chest. "Julia is worried. She says you don't look well."

"I've walked half the night and slept the rest on the floor of an abandoned cottage. How does she suppose I'd look?" Sage snapped. He cringed immediately at the bitterness in his voice. Julia reported to Basil out of concern for Sage. "My apologies, brother. It's been a…difficult night."

"Tell me what happened." To some it might sound like a sharp command, but Sage knew his brother worried. This attack involved Julia's sister. After discovering what Drake had done, Basil worked non-stop with Julia and Sage to see all rectified. The curse Drake placed over Marianne must be lifted.

Sage reported the events of the prior evening, with the exception of the incident involving his hand at the ball, as well as the manner of how he chased the bandits away. He also excluded the detail of the cottage catching fire and burning down. And those memorable intimate moments with Marianne.

Other than that, he told all to his brother.

When he finished, Basil remained silent, deep in thought.

After a few moments, he said softly, "Is that everything?"

"Yes," he lied.

"Very well. I'll leave you to your bath. We'll talk later."

Sage chose not to respond but heard the door gently close. He leaned his head back and shut his eyes. He sighed with contentment as the hot water eased his weariness.

"Do you need something, Marianne?"

There was only a moment of silence before she responded to his query.

"Does it bother you that I'm here?" Her voice came from the doorway. He'd smelled her lavender scent after his brother entered.

"No." His eyes remained closed, his head tilted back against the rim of the tub. He felt her presence as she walked around him, keeping against the wall for privacy's sake, until she could view his face.

He didn't understand how it was possible that he knew at every moment where she was located when in a room with him. He sensed her, felt her presence as if she were a part of him.

"Why did you not tell him of the fire?"

"I do not wish to burden him."

"Have you told no one then?"

Sage's teeth clenched. He wanted to tell Basil. If he told Basil, however, he'd need to explain what had happened in Drake's castle the night they rescued Marianne's body. That he wouldn't do. Not yet.

"No," he said.

"Your nightmare," she said her voice soft, not a whisper, just a gentle sound like a butterfly's wings brushing his cheek. "You may share it with me if you wish."

She wanted to help. Her sincerity touched him, but if he could not burden Basil with his troubles, he certainly did not wish to lay them on anyone else. Especially not Marianne with her sweet offer to unburden his soul. But avoiding her questions had led her here. He had to answer, provide some explanation, otherwise she would continue hounding him. She was relentless in her pursuit to help people.

"I try not to think of it." It was a simple enough answer, the most honest he could provide.

"Aunt Petunia says a person should talk of the things that trouble them. It takes the weight off your soul."

The corner of his mouth tilted in a grin. "Aunt Petunia says many things. Most of her advice is wise."

"I'm willing to listen. No matter how horrible."

"I know." Sage released a deep breath, letting the air escape his lungs. "I…"

He hesitated. The intelligent part of his brain told him he needed to discuss this with someone, but the emotional part of him was terrified. If he spoke of it, he couldn't pretend it was a dream any longer. A horrible, terrifying dream.

Not to mention the images still haunted his

memory. Images of a doppelganger Marianne with flashing fire in her eyes.

"I cannot," he said. "I'm sorry."

"Don't be. When you are ready, I am here."

"I'm not sure you are the one I need to speak to of this."

The silence that followed made his heart freeze in his chest. He'd hurt her, just now. With that simple statement he wielded a verbal dagger and stabbed her.

But how could she know what disturbed him? How could she know how he felt about her?

She couldn't know. She was so young.

A child.

No, not a child. She was a woman. A woman trapped and vulnerable. He refused take advantage of her in such a way. He was the only male in residence able to communicate with her. The time they had spent together during these last few months had only brought him closer to her, more willing to see the goodness in her heart. She was spirited, a delight to talk to, and those moments when they were apart made him yearn to be with her.

"There are some things I just cannot tell you," he said, trying to soften the blow.

"No need to explain, Sage," she said, her voice remaining calm when he thought she might be ready to spout fire.

He opened his eyes.

She sat in the corner of the room, her gaze fixed on his face. Like an angel with her hair cascading down her back in sensuous curls. He wanted to touch them, to find out if they felt as silky as he remembered.

She was his friend, but he wanted more from her.

More than she could provide.

His thoughts drifted back to the cottage. When he heard her screaming his name, he thought the highwaymen had returned, that she was being attacked. He hadn't realized he was the cause of her screams. The fire had destroyed every inch of the cottage. By sheer luck, it had not spread to the surrounding forest, otherwise...

Well, he'd rather not think of otherwise. When he saw her struggling on the floor of the cottage, reaching blindly in the smoke and fire to find him, he cursed himself a dozen times and more. She risked her life to save him. He, who was seemingly immune to fire.

And then he carried her from the cottage, pulled her as far as he thought safe and lay beside her on the road. He stared at the blaze and hated himself.

This could have been Merriweather Manor.

Sage was a danger to those he loved. If Sage couldn't find a way to break this curse, to stop the fires from consuming him, then he had few options left to keep everyone he loved safe.

And while the cottage burned, Sage had looked at her. The fear in her eyes struck his vulnerable heart. He drew her close to comfort her, happy he could at last offer physical comfort to her. He held her until she pulled away to search his face.

The moment he glimpsed her eyes, he knew the direction her thoughts had turned. When her gaze flitted down to his lips, heat stirred his blood.

She wanted to kiss him.

And suddenly he needed to kiss her, too.

But he'd pushed her away. He had to. He was dangerous. If she grew close to him, he would bring her pain. He must put a stop this. Stop her from coming to him when they weren't working together. Stop her from spending so much time with him, when he needed her to stay away.

"Do you ever wonder why I never propositioned you?" Sage asked, the anger in his soul making him lash out. "I've been with many women. They call me the Merriweather Rake, did you know?" He laughed at the absurd moniker the ton had dubbed him. "Yet you are the only one I've never seduced."

She flinched.

He thought the pain spreading across her face would make him feel just in his cause. He needed to push her away. From the look on her face, he succeeded. Instead of the satisfaction he thought it might bring, he felt only pain.

Pain from her sadness, her suffering.

"You are a good man, Sage," she said with a slight tremor in her voice, the only sign she was affected by his cruel words. "Do not fool yourself."

She stood and walked away.

The lavender scent faded. Sage rubbed a hand over his eyes, trying to block the image of her sadness from his mind.

Had he done the right thing?

This curse confined Marianne to a select few. Essentially, she was forced to speak with him, spend time with him, even just for the pure sake of her sanity. What choice did she have when no one else could hear or see her?

Marianne was not to blame for the fact that Sage's feelings regarding her were changing, that when he looked at her he saw not a child with gangly limbs, but a woman full-grown. One who had become a close friend. And that he desired their friendship to grow into something much more...intimate.

Was he a fool to punish her for his own misgivings?

Sage heaved a heavy sigh, then slapped the surface of the water since he had nothing else nearby to strike. The water sloshed over the rim.

Since the bathwater had cooled and any therapeutic effects it might once have owned vanished, he stepped out of the tub. After he dried and dressed, he went out in search of Marianne to make his apologies. He couldn't push her away. Instead, he needed to restrain his own growing emotions. No need to burden her with any more troubles. Who else could she speak with other than him? Only Julia. He could not imagine the invisible prison she suffered. He'd not make it worse for her.

He wandered the hallways, searching each room until he found her.

Well, in a manner of speaking.

He thought to check the yellow room in the east wing, hoping she might have retreated there to lick any wounds he had inflicted.

Although her body was in the room, her spirit was nowhere to be found.

He approached the bed where they had neatly laid her body. To the untrained observer, Marianne could be sleeping. Her chest rose and fell, indicating she breathed still. A rosy color kept her cheeks pink with life. He reached out and took her limp hand in his, feeling the warmth of her skin.

She was no corpse. Merely sleeping. A deep, deep

sleep. And she could not wake without her soul.

He watched her soulless body sleep for several long minutes. Her copper-tinted lashes fell gently over the creamy skin of her cheeks. Her pink lips curved delicately upward to give the appearance that she might be smiling ever so gently at some happy thought or dream. The unruly curls of her red hair still begged to be tamed even as she rested peacefully in the bed. He lifted a few strands off her shoulder, rubbing them between his thumb and forefinger. It felt like the most precious silk.

Although she rested in front of him, sleeping the deepest sleep, Sage felt alone.

Marianne wasn't here.

Her vivacious smile and indomitable spirit were nowhere to be found in this room.

An ache emerged in his chest. It wasn't painful. But he was aware of it. It had happened before, although he tried to ignore it.

What was it? This feeling of wanting to be near Marianne? Of the hollowness he felt inside whenever she was absent from his side? Of the yearning that occurred making him wish to seek her out? Of the sense of completeness that overcame him whenever she stood near to him?

When had it happened?

When had he fallen in love with Marianne?

He groaned, the angst-filled sound echoing in the empty room. He dropped her hair and rubbed at his eyes when drops of moisture emerged from the corners.

How had it happened? How had he gone from regarding Marianne as a sweet younger sister to a loving, spirited companion?

"Ah, Marianne," Sage whispered, hoarsely. "If only I could help you. Save you."

The tingle at the back of his neck warned him that he was no longer alone. A waft of lavender reached his nose. The ache in his chest eased. Warmth filled him, and he smiled.

"You are helping me," she said.

"It doesn't seem to be enough."

"It will."

They remained silent for a few companionable moments after that, each lost in their own thoughts as they stared at the body.

"What did you mean..." Sage halted his words, uncertain whether to speak his thoughts aloud. "When you said I was your closest friend?"

He lifted his bowed head, turning to her. She stood by the doorway, her hand moving toward the frame as if she needed to grasp it to stand tall. Her fingers vanished into the wood. She yanked her hand to her chest, clutching her fingers into a fist.

"Well, you are," Marianne admitted. If she were corporeal Sage imagined her face would flush a shade of red to match her hair. "I'm forgotten by most everyone. You are the only one who pays attention to me."

"Julia and I remain the only two who can *see* you, Marianne."

"No, no, it's not that." She waved her hand in protest. Then her gaze locked on something of extreme interest on the wall beside him. "Even when I was a child...Well, with eight years separating us and my mother dead, Julia treated me more as a daughter than a sister. Your family, too, found ways to convey their feelings for me. I was the neighbor girl, a child who ran rampant among the estate. But you…"

She paused to gather her thoughts. Sage remained silent, watching her, wishing again he could hold her hand.

"You *listened* to me. You talked to me as an equal, not a child. You teased, made me laugh, played games with me when the others were too busy to be bothered. You were not simply my neighbor, you became my friend." She shrugged her shoulders. "Even Julia never found time to play games with me."

Her memories took him back to when they were children. The gap in their ages remained as distant as Marianne and her sister. Unlike his siblings however, Sage never let that stop him from being entertained by the impish ginger-haired girl. His memories always included mischievous smiles, bouncing red curls, and contagious laughter. Marianne was fun. And her antics never ceased to amuse him. So while the other Merriweathers found entertainment elsewhere, he'd sought out Marianne's company.

And what she said was true. They had become friends, despite the difference in age. Even after adulthood crept upon him, whenever Sage returned home, he was always pleased to find Marianne bouncing into the hall to greet him.

Perhaps, his growing fondness for her began long ago. Deep in his heart, he'd found a companion in Marianne because they were alike. Ready to tease, to joke, to laugh, to amuse. No one else could tease a smile from him like Marianne. Even when he felt his most churlish, one smart comment from her would turn his mood.

He just never noticed the difference between Marianne and every other woman.

Marianne had grown into a beautiful woman, there was no denying, but underneath the skin...No one could compare to her.

"We've always been great friends, have we not?" Sage smiled.

Her gaze returned to his. She nodded her agreement.

"And so it will remain," he said softly, resolved. His growing desire for her would never conflict with their friendship. He could not bear it if he succeeded in pushing her away as he'd considered. Instead, he'd restrain his affections toward her, retaining her as friend, not the lover his heart was imagining her to be.

After all, Marianne was engaged to that Fernsby fellow. Fernsby was of an age with her. Sage was too old. How could she possibly think of him in any romantic way? He was a fool.

But Marianne did not smile in return. She continued staring at him, her eyes so wide they seemed almost owlish.

Was it too late? Had Sage pushed too far? Perhaps Marianne did not wish to continue their long-term friendship.

He frowned when she turned to walk away. His chest tightened, as if an invisible force squeezed so he could not breathe.

"Marianne," he said a note of panic in his voice. She halted in her tracks, then looked in his direction. "Will you sit with me while I sleep? Wake me if I...dream again?"

"Of course," she said. "I planned to do so whether

you liked it or not."

Relief filled him. Despite his intentions, he hadn't pushed her away. She was his friend still. And they would remain friends. Sage would see to it.

He needed a friend now more than ever.

Marianne would watch over him while he slept. He couldn't bear it if he caused another fire.

Chapter Eleven

Something was different about Sage.

Marianne stood in a quiet corner in the ballroom, observing Sage as he danced with the homely Miss Caruthers. He laughed charmingly at whatever comment she made, making her face light with admiration. By all outward appearances, Sage Merriweather remained the handsome gentleman rake he was always known to be. No one in this room could distinguish a difference between this man today versus the man he had been a week ago.

But Marianne knew.

Sage had withdrawn.

He was quiet, reserved.

Solemn.

He didn't seek her out as often as he once had. Something had changed him.

Was it the fire at the cottage?

Since he refused to talk about the incident, she assumed that was what kept him subdued. He feared the fire magic he possessed and his lack of control.

He requested her presence just once, but Marianne visited his bedchamber every night. She watched while he slept. And though he never had nightmares as frightening as the night at the cottage, he suffered them still.

Each night he tossed in his bed sheets, tangling

them in his limbs. Once he fell to the floor as he fought whatever attacked him in his dreams.

Marianne did not speak to him of the dreams. She trusted that he would tell her when, or if, he was ready.

Sage appeared recovered from his ordeal with the highwaymen and cottage, enough so Basil agreed not to accompany him to this meeting tonight with the mysterious Desmonda Green. She had sent a missive several days prior, announcing her intentions to attend the Carutherses' ball. It said nothing more.

Marianne's gaze drifted from Sage to the many faces gathered in the ballroom. This affair was not the crush they had endured last week. She had no difficulty avoiding contact with people when she walked among the participants searching for the ginger-haired half-demon.

She searched for a full hour before coming to stand in the corner next to a huge potted plant.

The song ended, and Sage performed the last movements of the dance with Miss Caruthers' hand lightly placed on his arm. Marianne's chest tightened with envy. The young Miss Caruthers was not aware of her good fortune, to be able to touch Sage in such a manner. For the last week, Marianne gritted her teeth with frustration in her predicament. Her thoughts kept circling around the brief kiss she and Sage shared. Her lips burned at the memory.

"Bloody hell," she whispered, rubbing her lips. Perhaps the only good to come of her seclusion from the world was that she could utter all the swear words she ever overheard from the Merriweather boys. Only with Sage and Julia present did she need to guard her tongue.

"Bloody, bloody hell." She spoke louder this time since Sage was too far away to reprimand her for it.

As if he heard her speak, his head turned. His gaze locked with hers. His smile faded.

Marianne pressed her lips together to keep from swearing again, lest he discover what she mumbled. What was it about her that made him so unhappy? Ever since the night in the cottage, a barrier of some sort had been built between them. He seemed so serious around her. Like all the laughter had left his soul.

Perhaps it wasn't reaction from the fire magic. He'd suffered that ordeal since returning from Castle Blackmoor where he helped rescue Julia, Basil and her own body. Several months after, Sage continued with his jesting and jovial attitude, behaving as though nothing dreadful had occurred. He'd masked it. Hiding his frightening secret, so as not to burden those who loved him.

This was different.

It was as if he'd given up on something.

But what?

Another song began. Another dance partner for Sage. His attention torn from her as he focused on a new woman whom Marianne did not recognize at first. As she peered closer, she recalled the lovely Mrs. Watson. She often saw Sage in this woman's company. In fact, Marianne suspected she and Sage were lovers.

The thought made her queasy. She knew Sage was a rake. If the rumors were true, he had taken many lovers. The ton referred to him as the Merriweather Rake, after all. But Marianne made it a point not to discover the truth of those rumors. It was enough to imagine what he did at night. She need not witness it for herself, even if she could walk undetected through walls.

The couple twirled upon the dance floor, the cloth of the numerous colorful gowns floating like clouds of rainbows surrounding them. Marianne's fingers clenched into a fist. Oh, how she wished to dance!

With Sage...

His name presented itself in her mind. Warmth crept up her ghostly skin. She had danced with Sage a few times before the curse was placed upon her. It was nothing extraordinary. He was a competent dancer, never stepping on her toes or holding her hand too tight. Why did the thought of dancing with him now make her heart beat just a bit faster in her chest?

Marianne swore again. At this rate, she'd begin speaking like a sailor if she didn't watch her tongue.

She tried dragging her attention from Sage and his pretty partner. She had better things to do than observe him dance. She *should* search for Miss Green. After all, they needed to speak with her. It was imperative they discover what assistance she could provide.

And, yet, Marianne's feet did not move. She remained rooted beside the hideous potted plant shoved into the corner of the room, probably to keep it hidden from the guests' vulnerable eyes. Instead of searching the house where Sage could not traverse, Marianne remained in the same room.

Watching him.

Imagining what it would be like to dance with him...to be held by him...to kiss him again...

She sighed and looked away.

"....Marianne. I hope she never returns."

The sound of her name caught her attention.

Marianne recognized the voice of her friend, Charlotte Smythe. She scanned the crowd until she found her friend's familiar brunette hair pinned with decorative flowers matching her dress. Charlotte stood a few steps from Marianne, sipping a glass of ratafia. Maria Spaulding stood next to her, smiling and nodding in agreement.

"It would make things less complicated."

"I suppose he wouldn't mind, would he?" Charlotte took another sip from her glass before lowering it to add, "After all, what good is a fiancée who cannot be found?"

"Did he really tell you they were promised to each other?" Maria asked, lowering her voice. She tilted her head toward Charlotte, who was several inches shorter.

Something of the gleam in Charlotte's eyes made Marianne uneasy. She moved closer to better hear her response. She had mentioned her name, after all. Why was she speaking of her?

"A secret engagement," Charlotte whispered loudly. "Known only to the two of them. And, myself, of course. Apparently, he thought himself madly in love with her when they first met. But that was an entire year ago…"

"And then she disappeared," Maria finished for her friend.

A sick feeling grew within Marianne's stomach as she stopped to stand next to Charlotte. She could touch her friend without Charlotte having any knowledge of it.

"He reconsidered his feelings shortly after. Dear Mr. Fernsby tells me as soon as she's returned to England he's to inform her of his intentions. Her behavior toward him has been horrid and unbecoming. She should dare to abandon him for so long? If he'd known she had no plans to honor her promise to wed, he never would have lost his heart in the first place. Instead, he'll have mine, as soon as we wed next spring."

"It does make it all the easier if she doesn't return. Let her stay in Belgium or wherever they say she is. Since neither has mentioned their engagement to anyone, he can call it off with no one the wiser."

"If she fails to return until next year, she'll have the surprise of a lifetime to discover her fiancé wed to another!"

"It's no more than she deserves. After all, she always was a bit queer. The lot of them from Meryton, if you ask me. The Merriweathers are so…odd. Well, all save the present Mr. Merriweather. He's there now, dancing with Harriet Watson. She's a great beauty, is she not? And she fancies him. She told me he made advances to her a week ago. Mentioned the possibility of a union. It's a marvelous match. Harriet will make a perfect wife…"

"No," Marianne said.

She wasn't certain for a moment which part of Charlotte's revelation she protested. That Charlotte was planning on marrying *her* darling David, or that she suggested pretty Harriet would make a perfect wife for Sage. Either held disastrous appeal. And Marianne would not stand for it.

"They say he's favored Mrs. Watson ever since her husband died at Waterloo. He comforted her during her time of grief, and they grew close. They've formed quite an attachment."

"No!" Marianne repeated, shouting this time. "Do not speak such scandalous lies!"

Heat rose swiftly to her cheeks, startling her with its intensity. It shocked her still that her spirit form reacted as her body might. Her heart rate increased with speed of the swelling anger from the inability to *do* anything to stop Charlotte's plans.

"How could you say such horrid things? I thought you were my friend!" Marianne screamed at Charlotte now. What did it matter? No one could hear her.

Tears welled in her eyes as Charlotte laughed at something Maria said. Standing there, sipping her ratafia…plotting to steal her fiancé…proposing to marry Mrs. Watson off to Sage.

"It will not happen!" Marianne shouted. "It will never happen! I won't let it, do you hear?"

Of course, Charlotte did not hear.

Marianne growled, an entirely unladylike sound, then clenched her fingers into fists and swung at Charlotte. If only she had substance to inflict the pain tearing through her heart. She aimed for her friend's face. As she knew it would, her hand slipped through Charlotte's body, sending a shiver of electricity through her. Marianne swung once more, slashing her hand through Charlotte's shoulder before she stopped.

Charlotte shivered. "Oh, do you feel that cold air? I believe there must be a draft. Odd for this time of year, do you not agree?"

Tears pooled in Marianne's eyes as she glared at her former friend. If only she could do something to make her displeasure known.

"Is something the matter?" Sage's voice inquired from behind the group of ladies.

Marianne spun. He looked directly at her, his brow furrowed. Her heart leapt. He acknowledged her when no one else would...*could.* She bit her lip when she noticed the thunderous expression cast over his features. Was he concerned...or angry? He appeared rather furious.

Marianne glanced away.

"Nothing a walk in the garden would not alleviate," Charlotte said, obviously assuming Sage spoke to her. Marianne knew Charlotte smiled in delight at Sage's attention from the cheerful sound of her voice. "It's a bit chilly in here. Strange, don't you think?"

"Not at all. These old houses tend to be drafty." Sage said. His voice sounded...strained. Disappointed. He must have seen Marianne's fit of rage. Embarrassment replaced the angry heat in her cheeks. She had reacted like a spoiled child. Unbecoming of a young woman, even though she knew her actions would harm no one.

"Then will you not walk with me, Mr. Merriweather? We shall warm ourselves with the summer air."

"I admit, I cannot. My presence is promised to someone else at the moment. In fact, I must speak with her now. Good day to you, Miss Smythe."

"Yes, of course," Charlotte muttered, the regret clearly heard in her voice.

Marianne glanced warily at Sage. Again, he focused on her. She saw the swift tilt of his head, indicating she should follow, then he turned abruptly and walked away.

Marianne stifled the urge to run in the opposite direction. She did not look forward to this interview.

Her behavior had been that of a selfish child, and it embarrassed her that he was a witness to it. But even now she held her fists clenched at her sides with a strong desire to smash Charlotte's dainty little nose.

That she would betray her…

Her friend…

Marry David…

Mrs. Watson and Sage…

Marianne squeezed her eyes shut to squelch her tears. She swiped her wet cheeks to dry them. After taking several deep breaths, she pushed through the crowd to follow Sage as he led her out of the ballroom. Upon entering the corridor, she caught sight of him ascending the stairs. He glanced at her, checking if she followed.

The urge to spite him nearly overpowered her common sense. She wanted nothing more than to run and hide away. To sulk. Marianne was quite adept at sulking.

Perhaps he didn't wish to lecture her. It was something she was accustomed to from Julia. But Sage had never been one to behave so paternally, so she should fear no lecture from him. Yet lately, his behavior did baffle her.

So she followed. If he began with a sentence such as *"What were you thinking?"* as Julia was wont to do, Marianne vowed she'd turn around and walk out the door.

She followed him into an empty bedchamber. She stifled a giggle. If anyone knew she willingly entered a bedchamber with the Merriweather Rake, they'd hang! Then he'd be forced to marry her.

Her heartbeat quickened at the thought of Sage

being forced to propose to her. Indeed, she should be sickened by the thought. He was as a brother to her. Her friend.

And she was in love with David.

Was she not?

Thought of marriage to Sage did not sound so unappealing. A mixture of emotions stirred in her chest, but she could not think upon that now.

He was waiting.

She stepped fully into the room, then watched him close the door. He turned to face her.

"Are you all right?"

It warmed her to hear the concern in his voice. He did care for her...as a surrogate brother should.

"Yes."

"What did she say?" The thundercloud appeared over his features, taking Marianne by surprise. He did not immediately condemn her for her actions, but he *was* angry.

"Several things," Marianne muttered, glancing at the empty fireplace. "Where shall I begin?"

"At the end. The beginning. Anywhere," he said, taking a step toward her. "Just tell me what she said to anger you so."

Marianne's gaze flashed to his. Did his voice tremble? She stood transfixed. The myriad of emotions raced through her again as he stepped closer. He raised his hand, reaching for her cheek, then stopped.

A glimmer of pain passed over his features. He clenched his hand, pulling away.

"Tell me why you were so upset?" He whispered the words. Marianne heard them, but she stood spellbound by the look on his face. He had never seen her behave in such a violent way.

He was her friend. Of course, he would be concerned if she were made to be upset.

She shook her head, trying to snap out of the spell she found herself caught in as she gazed into his eyes. She blinked several times before finding words to answer him.

"I-I…she…She said you…," Marianne stuttered, struggling to form a coherent sentence. What had Charlotte said to enrage her?

Sage was to marry Mrs. Watson.

Marianne swallowed hard as she recognized the truth. It wasn't the revelation that David planned to break off their engagement. That part had surprised her, but it hadn't elicited the rage that struck to cause Marianne to lash out.

It was the part about Sage planning to marry Harriet Watson.

Marianne never expected Sage to marry. They called him a rake. Rakes did not marry. But Sage was different, was he not? Although he behaved as a rake in public, in private she knew him better. He was kind, thoughtful, caring. A gentleman of the highest order. He deserved to marry. To have a family. To be happy.

But Marianne did not want him to marry…

It was pure selfishness…this feeling of not wanting Sage to marry. What sort of friend was she that she did not wish him to have the same happiness her sister now shared with her husband? Marriage would do well for Sage. She could easily envision him happily wed to some beautiful, talented woman who would gift him with dark-haired children with the most amazing blue eyes.

Her stomach clenched. She felt ill.

No, she did not want Sage to marry anyone, except…her.

This knowledge should have shocked her. It should have sickened her. How could she feel this way about Sage? Her neighbor and long-time friend?

She was not immune to his many charms, it was true. But he never played the rogue in her company. The part he played in society was not the way he behaved toward her. With his close friends and family, he was himself.

She loved him.

Calm rushed over her. As if she had denied the truth for ages and now after admitting it finally, peace descended upon her.

But she could not tell him. He would despise her for it. What a horrid way to ruin their friendship.

He awaited a response. She had to tell him something to explain her behavior.

"David wants to break off our engagement," Marianne said, the words spilling from her mouth.

A flicker of…something dashed across his features. He looked away before Marianne could identify it.

"She said this?"

Marianne nodded. "She claims he wants to marry her. They plan to wed next spring."

"Do you believe her?"

Marianne closed her eyes. "Perhaps," she admitted her voice soft. "I haven't had word from him for quite some time. And last week I hadn't the chance…"

Sage's hand catching on fire had ruined any chance to listen to David speak at the party they attended. Perhaps Charlotte was being overly optimistic in her assumptions that David planned to break it off with her.

But now…

Marianne did not wish to marry David. Her heart did not thump madly whenever she thought of him. Nor was he in her constant thoughts. Her love for David faded to tenderness. She cared for him still, but as a friend.

Where it had faded with David, it had grown with Sage.

Could it be she was fickle enough to fall in love with Sage simply because he was the only male able to speak to her? She paused to consider the thought. But Sage spoke again so she decided to think about it later.

"Do you love him, Marianne?"

She took a deep breath. She could lie to him. But if she did, would he know the truth? Would he see the love shining in her eyes was for him? No, she could not let him know. He would withdraw from her completely. Marianne couldn't imagine how she'd survive Sage's absence from her life. She needed him.

But did she need him only because she was condemned by this curse?

Better to lie to him now and learn the truth later.

"Yes," she said, staring boldly into his face. She focused on his nose to avoid looking directly into his eyes. "I love him."

Sage, she whispered in her mind. *I love* you.

He stared at her for a moment in silence. She waited for him to acknowledge the truth. How could she mask her soul when he gazed upon her so intently? Again, something akin to pain flickered across his face. He turned away.

"Very well," he said. "I'll look into it."

He turned and walked to the door.

"Wait," she said. He paused with his hand on the doorknob. He looked back at her. "What do you mean?"

"I'll discover what his intentions are," Sage said simply. "If he plans to marry Miss Smythe or if he remains devoted to you, I'll know of it."

"How? Our engagement was never declared. It was kept secret until I could discover a way to tell my sister. And to explain about our family to David. Most witch families do not marry outside our community. It's been too dangerous to do so in the past."

"It is not unheard of," he said. "My father was not a witch."

"No, he was a scholar. A man of education. Did he have difficulty learning the truth of your mother's abilities? Of her family?"

Sage frowned. "I suppose he was a bit shocked. But he loved her. He accepted her."

"There are many who would not."

"Do you think Fernsby among these?"

Marianne hesitated for only a moment. "No. Not David. Not if he loves me."

"Very well," Sage said. His jaw clenched as he looked away. "I'll discover the truth for you, Marianne. I promise." Then he opened the door and walked out of the room, leaving her to stare after him.

Another promise.

Many months ago Sage had promised to find a way to end this curse. Had he done it? Not yet. But he hadn't relented. Marianne had little hope, but Sage's persistence rallied her.

They would find a way to break this curse. And

when they did, Marianne would know for certain whether or not her feelings for Sage stayed true.

Chapter Twelve

Sage danced and danced. The faces of his many partners became a blur. And while he danced, Marianne searched. He watched her from the dance floor, catching glimpses of her moving through the crowded clusters of matronly women and hopeful debutantes as they gossiped along the sidelines.

At several moments during the course of the evening, Sage had doubts as to whether or not Miss Green would make her promised appearance at the Carutherses' ball. Nearly an hour after Marianne's incident with Charlotte Smythe, Miss Green's stunning red hair caught his eye as she entered the ballroom. She scanned the dance floor. When she spotted him she smiled.

A chill crept up his spine at the sight. It was a predatory smile, to be sure. The knowledge that she had demon blood worried him, but he rallied himself, knowing the only path to save Marianne might lie within this woman's grasp. He would not give up until the spell cast over Marianne was broken.

The song ended just as Desmonda Green advanced into the room. She found her way through the small crowd until she stood in front of him.

"Shall we dance?" she asked, a seductive smile taunting her rouge-colored lips. The sight did little to arouse him. Instead, he thought of Marianne's spirited smiles and how differently these two women compared.

"I believe my card is full," Sage replied.

She laughed, taking his response as the teasing comment he'd intended it to be, but somewhere inside he'd been quite serious. He did not wish to dance with her. The mere thought chilled him. There was only one woman he wished to dance with, but a quick glance round the room revealed she was nowhere in sight.

Desmonda lifted a hand in invitation as the musicians prepared the next piece. Sage took her hand, leading her onto the dance floor.

"I thought you didn't wish to be seen with us," he whispered into her ear before they parted to perform the moves of the dance.

"Miss Grey is not here, is she?"

"Hereabouts." Again he searched the room, but noticed no sign of her.

"There is someone I want you to meet."

Sage's gaze lifted to the ceiling before returning to her. "I've heard this before from my brother."

"I know of only one way to help you, Mr. Merriweather, and I cannot do it alone. We'll need his assistance if you wish to break the curse."

"Anything to help Marianne," he muttered. "When do I meet him?"

"No," Desmonda said, frowning. "You misunderstand. Michael can help *you*, not Marianne."

Sage stumbled on a step, but quickly recovered. "And what of her curse?"

"Forgive me," she said, at a moment where she could lean close to him. "I know of no way to bring back the dead."

"She's not dead," he protested, disliking the way

those dreaded words lodged in his throat.

"But she is," Desmonda said. "This limbo will last a year. After that, her body will cease to breathe. Her spirit will travel into the afterlife. She will finally be at peace."

He stopped dancing. The couples around him tripped as they nearly collided. But he didn't move, just stared at her.

"Perhaps there is somewhere else we might speak?" Desmonda forced a smile to her lips as she glanced at the dancers around them. The unwanted attention seemed to make her nervous, but Sage could barely focus on anything other than her last words echoing in his mind...*her body will cease to breathe...her spirit will travel into the afterlife...she will be at peace...*

Desmonda tugged on Sage's arm, awakening him from his dazed state.

"My apologies," he said, as he noticed several sets of curious eyes staring at him. A shiver crept along his spine, as thoughts of his ancestors' fear of discovery flashed in his mind. Did the dancers overhear his conversation? They looked at him oddly, just now. Did they suspect he was a witch?

Reluctantly, he grabbed her hand and resumed the dance. No need to draw further attention themselves. Relief flickered across his partner's features as she relaxed back into the dance.

They performed the rest in silence, each with a forced expression of pleasure to ease the curiosity of any onlookers. When the music finished, he strode from the dance floor, her hand on his arm as he led her to the refreshment table. After he acquired drinks for them both, he found a quiet corner where they could speak in relative privacy. On the way, he kept searching the sea of faces for Marianne.

"There is a spell to break Marianne's curse," Sage said firmly. "Wherever there is dark, there is light. It's a lesson my aunt instilled in us since we were very young."

Desmonda shook her head gently. "If there is a spell, I know not of it."

"You must know someone who can help us. What of this man? This Michael? What sort of magic does he possess?"

"Michael knows of demon magic," Desmonda said. "I'm certain he can break the curse set upon you."

"Is he half-demon, like you?"

"No."

"And if he cannot break the demon's spell?"

"Then he can teach you how to use your magic."

"No. I won't accept that possibility. This is not my magic." Sage's voice lowered to a growl as he glanced briefly at his fingers. The memory of fire springing from them would haunt him for the remainder of his days. "But, for lack of a better word, my *infection* is not the reason Basil sent me to you. We were to help Marianne."

"Then I apologize, Mr. Merriweather. I have failed to assist you," Desmonda replied with a frown. "I did search, thoroughly, but all I found were myths and legends. Stories. The curse set upon her will reach its conclusion a year after it was cast. Then her body will wither and die. Her soul should be pulled into the ever after."

"*Should* be? You do not know?"

"I know of no one who has suffered this curse. All I know is the spell used to cast it. It was a lover's spell, used by the ancient spellcasters to discover what was called their *beloved*. My mother discovered a tale that claimed if the beloved was not discovered within a year, the cursed would sleep for a hundred more and awake reborn. Most likely it means after a year her body will die, and in a hundred years her spirit will be reborn."

"How does a beloved awake one cursed?"

"The lover's token from one who is true will undo what was once done." Desmonda's gaze lifted as she read the spell from her memory.

"Sounds rather cryptic."

"Most spells are written in such a way to stay hidden from discovery of those who are not magical," Desmonda explained. Sage understood. For centuries witches practiced their magic for the good of mankind, to cure the sick and discover truth in the world. But not all magic was perfect, nor were all witches of good heart. Occasionally, a witch might use a spell for nefarious purposes. Those few witches who turned to dark magic were the reason people hunted them throughout the world. And since there was no way to differentiate between a light and dark witch by appearance alone, the witch-hunters killed them all.

"So Marianne needs her lover's token," Sage replied, staring at the floor. "And what is that? A ring? A lock of hair? What?"

"It is but a story associated with the spell," Desmonda said. "It might mean nothing more than legend and lore. Without a specific spell or a potion, I don't believe we can help your Marianne."

At that moment, Marianne's ginger ringlets came into view. She stood at the edge of the area where the dancers performed a waltz. Whom was she watching so intensely? His gaze roamed over to the couples swirling around to discover the familiar visage of David Fernsby.

The man Marianne loved.

"…tomorrow, I know he will help cast the circle to perform the spell." Desmonda was speaking, but Sage had no memory of what she said. His attention focused solely on Marianne as she stared woefully at her beloved.

"I know I can help you, Sage," Desmonda said, touching his arm.

Sage flinched at the contact. He pulled his arm away from her, taking a step back to ensure she did not touch him again.

"I prefer never to be touched by a demon again," Sage snapped, rubbing his arm.

Desmonda's eyes widened.

Guilt assaulted Sage. Desmonda was not the demon who hurt him. He looked away. "My apologies. I—"

"No need," Desmonda interrupted. "I understand most interactions with demons are not…pleasant."

Sage said no more of the subject. Flashes of fire-lit eyes and hideous laughter still haunted his daytime thoughts to say nothing of the dreams he suffered at night.

"Meet me in two days. At dusk," Desmonda said, deciding to abandon the subject of demons. "At the church in Highston. Michael and I will await your arrival."

"Very well," Sage said.

With a brief nod, Desmonda Green took her leave of him. As soon as she walked away, he turned his attention back to Marianne.

She loved Fernsby. But did he love her? Sage vowed he'd have the answer before the end of the night. His gaze strayed to Mrs. Watson who, as luck would have it, was currently dancing with Mr. Fernsby. There was his source of information. Sage could always guarantee on Mrs. Watson's knowledge of famous gossip, even not-so-famous. He would discover her secrets before he approached young Fernsby. No need to frighten the poor fellow off. Marianne would never forgive him for that.

Marianne…

His attention returned to the forlorn young woman standing on the sidelines, watching her beloved dance with another woman. The sight pierced Sage's heart.

With a disgruntled sigh, he set the glass of sherry on a nearby table and went in search of something stronger to drink.

****

His methods of questioning differed from the average interrogation. Being a well-renowned rake, Sage always found seduction to be the perfect method of discovering what he needed to know.

Mrs. Watson was no different from any other woman of his acquaintance. After he approached, begging to have a private audience with her, she found no hesitation in locating an empty chamber on the upper floor. Sage had barely closed the door before she was pressed against him, her mouth attached to his, her arms clutching at his shoulders like dragon's claws.

There was, however, one complication he hadn't foreseen.

He did not wish to seduce or become seduced by Mrs. Watson.

"Harriet." Sage pushed her gently away. She suffocated him.

"What, my dear? Cannot wait for even a few kisses?" she asked, plunging her hand to his trousers to press her fingers against his flaccid member. "Well, this is an odd state of affairs at present. It can be remedied, I assure you," she added with a wink. Her fingers began working the buttons on his trousers as she knelt down in front of him.

"Not necessary, Harriet." Sage grabbed her arms to pull her back to her feet. She stood, looking at him curiously. He took several steps back, allowing distance to speak for itself. "When I said I have questions, I meant just that. Questions."

Mrs. Watson smiled, and then followed to where he stood near to the bed. "Of course, my love." She pulled his head down to hers, nibbling on his ear and whispered, "Afterward, I'll answer any such questions you put to me."

And then her hands roamed to the buttons of his shirt.

****

Watching Mrs. Watson dance with Marianne's alleged fiancé did little to improve her sour mood. Seeing Sage approach the woman afterward, then leave the room with her sent it spiraling further downward.

Was it true? What Charlotte claimed about them? That Sage planned to propose to Mrs. Watson? He never mentioned the woman's name aloud, nor any other woman in particular, come to think of it. So how could it be he planned to marry her? One would assume he'd at the very least talk of the woman he planned to wed.

Marianne chewed on her bottom lip for a moment, debating her course of actions. She'd already witnessed Sage speaking to Desmonda Green. The reason for their visit to this event was completed. So what purpose did he have leaving the room with Mrs. Watson? Why hadn't he come for Marianne and told her what information Miss Green had to convey?

Perhaps he…

Marianne's heart skipped a beat.

Perhaps he planned to propose to Mrs. Watson at this very moment.

Her feet were moving before she completed the thought in her head. She must stop him. Of all the women she knew—he knew—there surely must be a better choice than Mrs. Watson.

She'd glimpsed him ascending the stairs after he departed the ballroom. Wondering if he perchance took the woman to the same room where he spoke privately to Marianne earlier, she quickly took to the stairs.

Upon entering the room, she thought it empty. Then she heard a noise from her left and turned. Movement on top of the bed caught her attention.

Two people in various states of undress were writhing about on top of the coverlets.

Marianne froze.

In the past several months of her condition, she'd seen many things she was certain would make her sister swoon if she ever discovered. One of them was occurring right before her eyes. As a spirit, she had access to any such room, and the bedchamber was one of which she'd been mightily curious.

Truly, the sight of a couple making love had only created more controversy in her mind. Questions abounded, such as what did it feel like to be kissed so thoroughly? To be held with such passion? And why were people in such a hurry to strip down beyond their unmentionables if it appeared the very act itself was painful rather than pleasurable?

Marianne had seen the faces of the participants when they reached their conclusions. They contorted in rather pain-filled visages. She couldn't understand why they seemed so sated afterward.

The couple currently preparing for the act appeared in a state of hurry as the woman ripped the man's shirt from his chest. He tried to capture her hands, but she was too quick about it, and then she was kissing him quite thoroughly.

With all the movement between them in the shadows of the canopied bed, Marianne could not identify them until she heard Sage's voice.

"Stop, Harriet," he said.

Marianne gasped, then her hand flew to her mouth to smother the sound.

It was too late. He heard the noise.

Sage sat up, his surprised face appearing in the light of the candles.

"What are you doing here?" he asked Marianne, his voice rather breathless.

But she could not respond. She was stricken by the sight of him in bed with Harriet Watson. And she didn't have a moment to say anything, since Harriet obviously thought he was questioning her.

"I'm making love to you, silly man," she giggled. "Why else would you seclude me in an empty bedchamber?"

Marianne stepped back.

Sage attempted to stand, but Mrs. Watson's hands gripped his shoulders, drawing him back into the bed, back to her. He struggled for a moment, prying her claws from him until he was able to stand. His disheveled appearance might have amused Marianne at one time, long ago...before her feelings for him...changed, matured.

Instead, she was struck by two things rather simultaneously.

One...

An enormous amount of skin was revealed through the opening of his shirt as it hung at an angle unbuttoned across his chest. Marianne had difficulty removing her gaze from that particular area of his body. This was not the first time she'd seen him without his shirt, but that did little to stop her from gawking. There were lines, definition of muscle tone, something Marianne did not have on her body. Were men supposed to have such rigid bumps on their abdomens? She had assumed the bellies of men and women rarely differed. A belly was a belly, after all. Her own belly was rather soft, gently rounded. The last couple she'd witnessed in the bedchamber both had rather paunchy bellies, nothing that could compare to the view she currently witnessed.

As if he recognized the ogling of his clearly toned belly and chest, he straightened his crooked shirt, his fingers flying to refasten the buttons. The movement snapped her from the imaginings of what else he might have on his body worth taking note, and her gaze returned to his face.

Guilt shone in his eyes. In fact, he reminded her of a little boy who was caught at something he was told not to do.

Revealing number *two*…

Marianne loved Sage. She *loved* him. There could be no denying it.

The sight of him in another woman's bed created horrible emotions that twisted inside her soul.

Jealousy sang through Marianne. It poured from her fingers and toes, ate at her heart, clenched her stomach so tightly she thought she might be ill.

"This is not what it may seem…" Sage's voice trailed off. He swore softly when Marianne took another step away from him.

"Well, my love, what is it then?" Mrs. Watson asked, again assuming he spoke to her. "We were about to get closely reacquainted. You haven't shared my bed for over half a year now. I was beginning to believe you lost interest."

Marianne's gaze flashed to the woman who sat with her bare feet dangling over the edge of the bed. Her bodice had slipped revealing soft, creamy breasts, the nipples puckered.

Sage moved forward, bringing her attention back. She stood her ground, however, since if she took another step away she'd step into the wall. He dipped his head low to reach her ear and she closed her eyes as she imagined the feeling of his breath across her cheek.

"You shouldn't be here, Marianne," Sage whispered.

Marianne nodded. He was right. She shouldn't be

here. She should have minded her own business. If he felt the need to lie with a woman, who was she to interfere? She was nothing to him. Nothing. Oh, well, perhaps she judged too harshly. She was a neighbor. A friend. But nothing more.

And she was interfering. A pesky nuisance. The meddlesome little red-headed brat who always messed about underfoot when no one wanted her.

And it was clear Sage did not want her.

"I-I-I," Marianne stuttered, shaming herself further by revealing her lack of poise, sophistication. The knowledge that Sage slept with women, numerous women, should not shock her. Perhaps it did not shock her, since in the past she had teased him relentlessly over his pursuit of women. What else could she expect from the Merriweather Rake? But to see it so clearly right before her was another matter.

"Marianne," Sage whispered placing his hand on the wall above her, leaning over, his face so close all she could see was the blue of his eyes. So near again she imagined if she had substance she'd feel his warm breath on her skin. So close that her gaze darted to his lips with the desire to kiss him so he'd forget all those other women and think only of her. She was finding it difficult to breathe.

"I-I-I…"

She was a fool! Why could she not speak?

Tears sprung. Shameful tears. Tears of weakness, anger and hurt. Yes, hurt. Pain-filled her chest as she faced the knowledge that Sage would never kiss her like he kissed those other women. He'd never hold her. Caress her. Strip the clothes, even her unmentionables, from her body to lie naked in a bed. She'd never discover what happened to create such agonized expressions while screaming into the night. She'd never know what it was like to make love to him.

Marianne turned away. Then she took one last step into the wall and vanished.

Chapter Thirteen

Sage leaned his forehead against the wall where Marianne disappeared. Every muscle in his body urged him to run after her, to explain what she saw was a mistake. He had no intention of seducing Harriet. Indeed, he attempted to distract her when he heard Marianne's tiny gasp and knew they were no longer alone.

But he didn't move. Why explain? She had found him in quite the compromising position, but she knew who he was…*the Merriweather Rake*. Or who he had been. He doubted he could keep the gossipmongers going with that particular moniker since as of late he hadn't done anything rakish at all.

"Sage?" Harriet's voice reminded him that he was not alone.

"We're finished, Harriet," Sage said sadly. "I have no intentions of renewing our *acquaintance*, as you put it."

She was quiet for a moment. Then he heard the rustling of fabric. When he turned, he saw she'd readjusted her bodice to cover herself.

"You've fallen in love."

It wasn't a question, but Sage nodded.

"Ah," Harriet said. "I see. And does she…?"

"It's rather awkward business, I'm afraid. She's a friend and I—"

Harriet giggled. "My dear, Sage. Is it possible to be only *friends* with any female?"

He stepped back to the bed to sit beside her. He took her hand in his, placing a warm kiss upon her wrist.

"I hope you and I shall remain friends, Harriet."

"You are serious, are you not? You're in love? Well, this is a surprise, indeed," Harriet said smiling. She placed her hand over his. "Of course, my dear. Have we not always been friends? I knew some day you'd wish to marry. I never thought you'd be so foolish as to fall in love. So, now..." She released his hand to readjust her gown over her legs. "How may I help you?"

****

After speaking with Harriet, Sage searched for Marianne. But where does one go to find a ghost? Typically, one found ghosts in a graveyard, but he doubted highly to find Marianne there. And he could hardly ask anyone if they'd seen her. So he walked among the guests, searching and knowing he would not find her.

She was gone.

He could feel it.

David Fernsby had vanished, as well. He searched in vain, knowing the young man must have taken himself off home, despite the hour. Either that, or he'd found company elsewhere. Sage tried not to imagine what it meant for Marianne, despite Mrs. Watson's claims.

Perhaps Marianne was already on her way to Merriweather Manor. She used to escape to the gardens whenever she needed time alone, which for Marianne, was not often.

But he had no time to travel there tonight with his promise to meet Miss Green at the vicarage in Highston in two days. He'd never have time to keep his appointment since Meryton was in quite the opposite direction.

So instead of chasing after the headstrong girl, Sage left the Caruthers' house and found a hackney to take him to White's. He didn't visit the exclusive men's club often, but tonight he had need of the excellent brandy they provided.

A few hours later, he was deep in his cups, slouched in a comfortable plush chair and gazing at the drops of rain splashing the windowpane. It had begun raining about an hour ago. And all he could think of was whether or not ghosts got wet in the rain. If Marianne walked home, she'd be stuck in this downpour. Would she seek shelter?

He squeezed his eyes shut, trying to block out the image of her wet and shivering, and took another gulp of the brandy that left a sour aftertaste on his tongue. The drink didn't help him forget her, not even for a few hours.

So he had no taste for women or drink. What was he left with? What else to distract him?

He stood, thinking to make his way to the gaming tables. Perhaps losing a fortune would be enough to take his thoughts away from a pretty red-haired girl.

Instead, he found his feet stumbling down the steps as he departed White's.

"Steady, old boy," a voice said from below. A strong hand grasped his arm, keeping him upright. "Been a rough night at the tables, has it?"

Sage shook his head. "Not at all."

"On your way home, then?"

"Dunno," Sage slurred. "Wherever my feet take me, s'pose."

"Are you prepared to walk all the way in this weather?"

"Yes." Sage felt it only right he do so. After all, there was no shelter for Marianne on her journey home. If she need walk in the rain, he might as well.

"I'll walk with you then," the man said.

Sage squinted into the poor light of a lantern to identify his new friend.

"Lord Valentine." Sage attempted to stand a bit taller. He smoothed down his wrinkled vest and jacket. "No need to busy yourself, my lord."

"Nonsense," Lord Valentine said. "I was heading in the same direction when you stepped out."

Of course, Sage doubted it, especially in the rain, but since he didn't feel the strength to argue, he left it at that. They walked side by side for a bit, neither speaking as the small drops descended. Well, Lord Valentine walked, Sage stumbled a bit in a parody of walking. Lord Valentine's cane clipped at the cobblestones as they moved along, a rather gentle rhythm that soothed some of Sage's agitation.

Marianne could take care of herself. She was a ghost, after all. What harm could come to a ghost?

The image of a masked man flashed in his memory. The powder he had blown in her face, choking her. Then the man had touched her…

Before Sage knew what was about, he was kneeling in the bushes at the side of the street, dumping his guts onto the ground. When he finished retching,

Lord Valentine lifted him up and handed him a handkerchief.

"Come, old boy," he said. "Let's get you home."

The man turned him around and helped him ascend a carriage. It had the Valentine crest on the side. His driver must have followed them.

Sage closed his eyes as he sat on the cushioned bench, hoping the spinning taking place was only in his head.

He felt rather than saw Lord Valentine enter the carriage and sit across from him. There was a tap of the cane against the roof and then the gentle swaying of the carriage.

"Do try *not* to be sick on the upholstery," Lord Valentine said in a genial manner. "It's the devil to clean, I'm told."

Devil…*demon*.

The words brought an instant reaction. Sage's eyes opened. Lord Valentine sat with his hands folded on top of his cane. He saw him watching and smiled.

"Why are you helping me, my lord?"

Lord Valentine tilted his head as he considered the question. "How is your hand, Mr. Merriweather?"

Sage's fingers clenched into a fist, as though he might hide the unscarred flesh.

"You intrigue me, Mr. Merriweather," Lord Valentine continued when it became clear Sage had no intentions of answering. "And I feel a sense of responsibility toward you. You were injured at my party, after all."

"As you can see, I'm unharmed."

"That's what intrigues me," Lord Valentine said, leaning forward conspiratorially.

149

Witch-hunter.

It was a whispered word, even in his mind, but it brought Sage quickly to his senses. For centuries people had hunted his family and others like them. Simply because the witch-trials had ended, did not mean the hunting had. There were quiet, less public ways to rid the world of his kind. Was this man one of them?

"What do you want?" Sage asked. He tried to keep his fingers clenched onto the seat as he felt compelled to ready for a defense spell. He could not trust his magic to save him. It would only turn to flame.

"There was a carriage discovered not far from my house," Lord Valentine said, sitting back in his seat. "It was broken and burned. Seeing as how you had a previous...*incident* with your hand, I wonder; might you have any knowledge of how this occurred?"

Sage's heartbeat increased. He forced himself to appear relaxed instead of staring at the man across from him. He leaned back against the seat, taking a pose of nonchalance, although he was well aware of the carriage door to his right. He measured the distance in his mind, wondering how quickly he might reach it.

"No, my lord," Sage said, shaking his head. Of course, he wondered how adept Lord Valentine was at perceiving liars. There could be trouble between them if he did not take care with this conversation. He glanced beyond the carriage window, wondering how far they were from his London home, but all was dark.

"There was talk of it at one of the local taverns. Two men claimed to have seen a man caught ablaze. Fire sprouted from his fingertips, they said. But, no body was found. No evidence of this man who possessed the ability to control flame. Have you heard any of these rumors?"

Sage leveled his gaze with Lord Valentine's. "No."

Lord Valentine took a deep breath and nodded.

"Good. Since I did my best to squelch them before they spread any further. No need for such stories to cause an uproar. I had my men convince the locals they were the mad tales of a drunkard."

Sage's eyes narrowed. He remained silent, not certain whether he should comment. If there was no need to speak, it was better to stay silent so as not to condemn himself with any mistaken word. His head was still clouded with the after effects of drink. Lucky for him, brandy never loosened his tongue.

"You are correct with your assumptions that I want something from you," Lord Valentine said.

As he suspected. Sage waited for him to get on with it.

Lord Valentine leaned forward again, using the cane as leverage between them. "My brother left my house party shortly after you that night. As I understand it, he's caught up in some nefarious business. I—"

The man grimaced and paused, looking away from Sage for a moment as if to collect himself before he continued. "I'm told he attacked you on the road."

If the man had punched him in the jaw, he wouldn't have been more surprised. Lord Valentine's brother was the highwayman? Perhaps that's why he sounded so familiar. But it would mean the man was working for Drake. He had the powder he used on Marianne.

He knew about Marianne.

Did Lord Valentine know as well? Did he work for Drake, too?

Sage did his best to appear that this was an average, not-so-shocking conversation he was having with a friendly acquaintance, but the truth was he kept preparing scenarios in his head. If Lord Valentine acted against him, what were his defenses?

He'd not let anyone take him by surprise again. Sage had learned his lesson by his brother's hand. And just because his own magic had been stolen from him, the fire he possessed could be put quickly to use, as he proved with those highwaymen, although a tactic best used as a last resort.

"I don't condone his actions," Lord Valentine said quickly. He didn't notice Sage move his hands to his lap. "But no one knows of his whereabouts since that night. I need to know…"

Again the man paused to glance away. There was tension around his eyes. His fingers gripped the head of the cane so tightly his knuckles grew white. Perhaps he did not create this story. Was he telling the truth about his brother?

Sage imagined if Lord Valentine worked for Drake, there would be other ways to get him to talk. After all, Drake used demons for that. Sage tried not to flinch at the memory.

No, if Lord Valentine meant him any harm, he had ample opportunity to do so. He did not feel any danger coming from this man.

"Do you know what became of my brother that night, Mr. Merriweather?"

It was clear to Sage that Lord Valentine feared the worse for his brother. And the man had connected the burned carriage with his hand catching fire that same night. His injured hand that had not sustained any injury at all. It was guesswork. Purely assumptions, but Lord Valentine guessed correctly.

"I can tell you with all honesty," Sage said in a clear, steady voice. "I have no knowledge of what became of your brother, my lord."

Lord Valentine stared at him for a moment. Sage saw the doubt flicker in the man's eyes, but he kept his gaze on him.

"The truth?"

"It is."

"The stories the men told did not sound promising for my brother's welfare. The man they attacked threw balls of flame. I...have difficulty believing it, what they said, but after seeing your hand..." Lord Valentine let that last thought drift away. "You have your secrets, Mr. Merriweather. All men do. But, at last sight, I was told my brother was running for his life."

"Sounds like stories of frightened, drunken men. I would not believe every word they say," Sage said. It was the best he could offer. Even if he wanted to, he couldn't tell the man any more. He didn't know what became of the highwaymen after they attacked.

Of course, he didn't admit if not for Marianne's interference, Sage might have killed them.

The carriage slowed to a halt.

"Yes," Lord Valentine said softly. "I thought as much." He studied Sage for a brief moment, then leaned back into the cushioned seat. "I'm glad we had our little talk. And here we are, arrived at your address. Good evening, Mr. Merriweather."

Sage hesitated, not certain what else he should say. Words were no longer needed, however.

"Thank you, my lord." And he descended the

carriage. Upon entering his home, he scribbled a note for his servants to deliver in the morning. Not long after, he sank into the mattress of his bed, grateful for the exhaustion consuming him. With Marianne gone, there was no one to watch over him while he slept. But the drinking helped make him drowsy. No chance for dreams if he was too tired to think.

****

Sage relived it again. Caught in a loop, he returned to that night when he entered the mirror, traveling to Castle Blackmoor, to being locked in the room with the demon.

She twisted and curled around him, igniting parts of his body to watch him burn. He screamed in agony and fear. She bit him, licking his blood, drinking from him. He tasted his own blood as she tried to kiss him. Then there was pain again as the fire burned.

He screamed.

Soon the heat engulfed him. He wanted to die. To end the searing pain. He wanted an end to the scorching heat as it surrounded him.

And her laughter. Such an eerie sound. Hideous. Obscene.

She was morphing again, from Julia to Drake to Marianne. He tried looking away, but she wouldn't let him. She wouldn't leave him.

"Sage," she called. "Sage…"

She repeated his name over and over until he noticed the way she spoke his name. It wasn't with taunting laughter. It was with fear and panic.

"Marianne?" he mumbled.

"Wake up!"

She was screaming now. He blinked his eyes open,

realizing he was dreaming.

Or was he? Flames licked at his skin, his clothes, his hair. The bed sheets he lay upon burned. Smoke drifted above him.

To his left Marianne screamed his name.

He sat up about to leap from the bed, but the fear in Marianne's eyes stopped him. She held out her hands to prevent him from continuing his actions. If he stepped from the bed, he'd bring the fire to her.

Sage fought to breathe, fought to regain control of his rapidly beating heart. The fire was part of him. He needed to extinguish it before it spread to the rest of the house.

He closed his eyes and summoned all the strength he possessed to stop the fire. He imagined the flames curling into a soft glare before dying into wisps of smoke. The heat surrounding him lessened until he felt a chill air brush his cheek.

His eyes flashed open. Marianne stood in front of him, her hand on his face, ghostly tears streaming down her cheeks.

"I thought you were going to die," Marianne admitted, kneeling on the bed.

The fire was gone. The bed sheets were singed beyond repair, but the bed itself remained intact.

"I feared I would not wake you in time. You were dreaming again...And screaming. Oh, Sage, you were screaming. I've never heard such screams. And I could do nothing!" Marianne took her hand away to cover her face as she cried.

"But you did," Sage said, leaning forward, wishing he could take her hand back to hold it to his cheek. Strange, but he liked the cold of her presence against his heated skin. The contrast soothed him, calmed him, excited him. When he felt the cold air, he knew she touched him. He could close his eyes, imagining the feel of her skin as she touched him.

He shook his head. The desire for her consumed him as much, if not more, than the fire did. If only he could reach for her…kiss her again.

"Marianne, do not cry," Sage said. "I cannot bear your tears, my love."

The word slipped from his tongue. It was an endearment, nothing more, he chided himself. How often had he used it before when it had no meaning? Now, however, the word held power. And he'd never use it regarding another woman for the rest of his life.

"Please, stop crying. You'll stain the linen with your tears, darling, not to mention your dress. How do you manage to keep your gown clean? Do you have ghostly servants whom I never noticed, keeping your wardrobe pressed and ready to wear?"

Sage's attempts to make her laugh didn't work. It was a poor attempt, he admitted, but she did stop crying so he called that small feat a victory.

She stared solemnly at him. The depth of her gaze alarmed him. What was going on inside her head that she looked at him so seriously?

"I'm sorry I did not follow through the mirror," she said after an eternity. "I'm sorry I was not there to help you."

The mirror taking them to Drake's castle.

To the demon…

"No," Sage said. All attempts at laughter vanished. He was in all seriousness as he stared back. "Never regret your decision. I told you to stay, and I thank the gods and goddesses that you obeyed. I could not bear it if you witnessed the horrors that took place there. Marianne, it was…"

He flinched, remembering who she was and what he was about to tell her. He couldn't. But he had to… He must tell someone. He was going mad keeping it to himself.

"What? What was it?"

"A demon attacked me," Sage said, before he could think twice of it. Saying the word aloud sent a chill through him, of a different sort than what he experienced with Marianne's ghostly touch. "I was chained against a wall. It came to me, changing its appearance several times. It did…horrible things."

Marianne's silence comforted him. She didn't run screaming from the room, which he quite expected of her. Instead, she sat next to him, quietly listening to every word he uttered. He decided to tell her more.

"It fed off my magic as I tried to attack it to free myself. It consumed my power and then me. It tasted my blood. And then used its fire magic on me. I watched my skin burn. I felt the heat tearing through my flesh. But even as painful as it was, my skin did not peel or blacken. It remained just as it is now."

He hesitated, hating the images that flashed even as he kept his eyelids open. Would it never stop?

"I thought I might die. I wish I had."

"No," Marianne said sharply. "Never say that. Never. You stayed alive. You had no choice. Your will is too strong, and I'm glad for it. I couldn't imagine if…"

Sage waited for Marianne to finish, but she stared off into the distance, her mind somewhere other than in this room with him.

"What?" he asked, needing to bring her back.

Marianne blinked. She turned back to him. "I couldn't imagine losing you."

He tried not to fool himself. That was not love shining in her glistening eyes. Well, perhaps it was love. The kind friends share. Not akin to the type of love he felt for her.

"I'm here," Sage said, smiling to reassure her. "Perhaps not whole. I'm cursed with its blood, Marianne. It's tainted me. That's what Miss Green meant. She sensed its claim upon me."

"But…how can it claim you if the creature is dead. Did you not say Julia killed it?"

"Yes." He nodded. "I suppose it matters not if the creature is dead. Miss Green intends to help. I need to meet her at a vicarage in Highston. Will you accompany me, Marianne?"

Marianne nodded. "Of course."

Chapter Fourteen

The vicarage at Highston was a crumbling bit of stone and mortar. It was an ancient structure and had seen better days. The church spire rose high into the night sky. Sage descended from the carriage he drove, Marianne alighting behind him.

He pushed open the church doors which creaked and groaned under the weight of years of service. Marianne crept in behind, coughing at the dust that stirred up.

"How can dust bother you? You have no substance."

Marianne waved the dust from her face as she tried to suppress any further coughs. "There's several things about my existence I do not understand." She tilted her head to observe the many cobwebs hanging from the rafters. "Is it abandoned?"

"It appears so." Sage noted the thick dust covering the fixtures. A lantern sat unused in the corner of a table. He struck flint to light it, lifting it to illuminate his way. The rows of pews stretched into the darkness, becoming visible only as he walked closer. Once at the dais, he saw what was left of the items the church used for their services.

"I don't see anyone," Marianne said, peering into the dark gloom surrounding them beyond the shelter of the light's glow.

"Nor do I."

"Perhaps we should look out of doors? She might be wandering the graveyard, searching for potential victims." Sage sent her an irritated glance. She saw his expression and shrugged. "Is that not what demons do?"

"Along with the haunting of ghosts…"

Marianne scowled.

"Just an observation," Sage said, his mouth lifting into a small smile. Even during this frightening time, Marianne could still make him smile.

Brilliant.

Marianne made a huffing noise and marched forward into the murky darkness. Sage followed, lifting the lantern high to illuminate her path. They found a side door. Opening the rusty hinges, creaking loudly, they found themselves outside among the buried dead.

Large and small gravestones littered the ground. Marianne picked her way about, scanning the edges of the dark. Outside the moon illuminated the area so they did not need the addition of the lantern, but Sage kept it in case they stepped farther into the wooded area behind the church.

Searching into the trees, he saw movement.

"Marianne," he whispered to alert her. She turned toward the direction of his gaze.

A flash of red appeared beneath a hooded cloak. As the figure stepped forward, pale hands drew the hood back. Bright red hair, much like flame in the moonlight, identified Desmonda Green.

The figure at her side, they did not know.

"You are late," Desmonda observed by way of greeting.

Sage glanced at Marianne.

"Fashionably so," he said. "Miss Grey required a seamstress for her attire."

Desmonda searched the space beside him, seeing nothing, she narrowed her eyes and returned her gaze to him. Sage smiled at the woman's consternation.

"I see we have a guest," Sage said, peering at the small unassuming man next to her.

"This is the Reverend Michael Blair," Desmonda introduced. "He's graciously agreed to assist us this evening."

He was of average height, perhaps as tall as Desmonda, with mousy brown hair and spectacles. As he moved, his cloak fell opened to reveal simple garb.

Sage should be accustomed to the extraordinary, but the sight of a clergyman keeping company with a half-demon surprised him.

"How do you do?" Mr. Blair muttered, reaching out to shake Sage's hand in greeting.

The tingle Sage felt upon contact surprised him, too.

"You're not quite human, are you?"

Mr. Blair flushed and sent Desmonda a quick glance. He cleared his throat before speaking. "No. I'm a witch...of sorts."

"A powerful sorcerer," Desmonda added. "Though he's shy of using his talents."

The reverend looked away, glancing at his feet, then Sage's feet, then the church beyond, keeping his gaze anywhere except on the faces of his companions.

"You look nervous," Sage observed.

Mr. Blair shrugged. "Rather uncomfortable, I'm afraid. Miss Green and I have an arrangement. I'd like

161

to get the ceremony finished so I might get back to my parish."

"By all means," Sage said. "What do we need to do?"

****

The Reverend Michael Blair and Desmonda prepared while Sage and Marianne stood back, watching. They each carried a pouch of white chalky dust which they sprinkled over the ground where they deemed a proper circle could be held. The graves of the dead littered the area, but none interfered with their movements. Desmonda said they needed the power of the dead for this spell. The way she spoke sent shivers along Sage's back, but he nodded in compliance. What could he do to argue, after all?

They created symbols on the dirt with their dust, sprinkling heavily over there, lighter here, until many strange designs covered a large area. After that, they closed the circle around the symbols.

Michael clapped his hands together, dust from his fingers puffing into his face until he choked.

"That's finished. Now, onto the next. Are you prepared?" He looked at Sage over his spectacles.

Did he have a choice? Sage shrugged his shoulders and nodded.

"What does he mean to do?" Marianne whispered from his side.

"I've no bloody idea," Sage whispered back.

"I need to know your connection to the demon," Michael said a moment later as he gingerly approached Sage. He took his spectacles off to wipe the sweat beading on his brow. "How did you meet? What did it do? That sort of thing."

162

Sage's face remained impassive, but with a glance at Desmonda and Marianne, he turned back to Michael.

"I'd rather not speak of it."

Desmonda stepped forward. "He needs to know certain details in order to perform the ceremony correctly."

Sage's brow arched. "No."

"Anything at all. Can you describe it? I cannot imagine it obliged you by giving its name. That would be too easy by far. But any pertinent details would be a blessing."

"Pertinent details?" Sage repeated.

Michael nodded.

Sage sighed. "It changed form at will. Female to male and back. It had power of flame. When it...attacked me, it absorbed my power. I couldn't use magic of any kind for several weeks after. And when I did begin to regain use of magic, it was tainted by fire. Now, every time I cast a spell it turns to flame."

Michael nodded. "I know this demon."

"You can summon it?" Desmonda asked.

Michael nodded again.

"Wait. What?" Sage took a step forward. "Summon it? You can't. It's dead."

The reverend heaved a deep sigh. "It takes incredible strength to kill a demon. Most often, it's cast back to Hell, back into the underworld. That's where your demon is residing."

"It's alive?" A chill crept along Sage's skin. The rest of Mr. Blair's statement crept into his brain. "You cannot summon it," he protested. "That magic is the blackest of its kind. And the demon is strong...terrifying..."

"If you have any hope of severing your bond, it must be dealt with, otherwise the connection with you will remain for as long as it pleases."

Sage took several steps backward, stumbling for a moment before placing his hands on his knees to steady himself. The demon was not dead…For all this time, he had considered his family safe, thinking the demon deceased. Imagining now, the creature had access to him at any time in the last six months created a wave of panic that stunned him. After a few moments of deep even breathing, he regained his equilibrium. Tonight, the ties between him and the demon would be broken. Straightening with clenched fists at his sides, he nodded.

"Very well."

"During the attack, did the demon take anything from you? A lock of hair, article of clothing?"

Sage shook his head. "Nothing of which I'm aware."

"Did it have contact with any bodily fluids? Did it kiss you or…?"

"Yes," Sage said abruptly. "It kissed me and bit my shoulder. She said she liked the taste of my blood." He cringed at the memory.

"Ah, that's it then. We'll need a few drops of your blood to complete to circle."

Desmonda pulled a small blade from a hidden compartment in her dress. She approached Sage, requesting his hand. A quick flick of her wrist and tiny drops of blood oozed from the cut on Sage's arm. He followed her around the circle, dropping his blood to complete the magic.

Michael faced the circle, reciting words from a

scroll he extracted from the bag at his feet. The words were in another language, one Sage was not familiar with. They felt ancient. As the reverend spoke, he sensed the power beginning to build. It rose from the ground, encircling them in a storm of magic. It was difficult to breathe.

Fear came with the magic.

Sage had been frightened when facing the demon before, but now he forced his feet to the ground when all he wished to do was flee. This was the blackest sort of magic. The sort that should never be attempted. And he was about to confront the demon who haunted his memory.

Within moments, flames burst forth around the circle, creating a ring of fire. Something dark and shadowy began to emerge from within the flames. A mass of dark clouds, coalescing into the shape of a dark-haired woman with flashing red eyes. As soon as she formed fully, she turned those demon eyes on Sage. A slow smile curved her lips.

"We meet again."

****

Her voice was a seductive purr, more animal than woman, more creature than animal.

"Show no fear," Michael shouted. Marianne hadn't noticed the rumbling that began when the magic started. The wind picked up, roaring around them like a giant thunderstorm. "It feeds on fear."

"Bloody brilliant," Marianne heard Sage mutter. Since she practically crawled up his arm in fright, she could hear him quite clearly. She took a moment to gather herself. Marianne was frightened, more than ever before, but she reminded herself this demon could do

165

nothing to harm her. She was already a ghost. How could anyone harm a ghost?

Marianne didn't hear Mr. Blair begin his exorcism. He shouted words at the demon, words she couldn't identify since it sounded much the same as the ancient language he had used to summon the demon.

The demon turned to the reverend, her smile sickly sweet on her beautiful face. She spoke to the man in the same language, growling the words. Her eyes widened at his response, and if possible appeared a brighter, angrier red. She lifted her head back and howled in rage, the fierce wind whipping her hair around her naked form.

Then she stopped, turned her head, pointing at Marianne.

"You," she said with the evil smile back in place. "I want you."

"What?" Michael appeared baffled. He looked at Sage, a puzzled expression on his face. "What do you mean?"

"Oh, no." Desmonda rushed toward them, grabbing Sage's arm in her hurry to reach them. Sage flinched, brushing her off. She released him with a quick apology. "You said Miss Grey arrived with you? Is she here now?"

"Of course," Sage said. "She goes with me everywhere."

Desmonda's eyes closed. Her lips moved in a prayer Marianne had heard before, one seeking protection. When the woman's eyes opened, grief and sorrow poured from her green gaze.

"Tell her to run!" Michael shouted.

"It will do no good," Desmonda said quietly.

"What's happening?" Sage asked with a worried glance at Marianne.

"Michael has bargained for your freedom. At the price of Marianne's."

"What?" Sage asked. The fury in that single word chilled Marianne, enough for what Desmonda said to sink into her brain.

"Tell her to run!" Michael repeated.

At his words, the demon surged against the circle. The flames shot up higher. Michael dropped the scroll he'd been holding, and Marianne saw his mouth move. Then he lifted his hands, pushing into the air. Vibrations echoed through the air, and a faint light pulsed from the reverend's hands. He was holding the demon back, keeping it trapped in the circle.

"Marianne, you must run. She doesn't have your blood scent. You must hide." Desmonda spoke into the air as she had no sense of where Marianne stood.

"Sage? What's happening?" Marianne's voice was a faint whisper. She stared at Desmonda like the woman was a creature she'd never before seen, one just as frightening as the demon now surging against the wall. Michael pushed against the barrier, attempting to keep the demon in its place.

"There's nothing more we can do," Desmonda said to Sage. "Marianne is vulnerable. Her body can be possessed with anyone who controls her spirit. Do you understand what that means? The demon can take over Marianne's body!"

"Come, Marianne," Sage said without waiting to hear more. He turned to run.

"No, wait!" Desmonda grabbed Sage's arm before he could take another step. "You cannot go with her.

The demon has tasted your blood. It can track you. It will take longer to find Marianne if she goes alone."

"Marianne," Sage said, turning to her. "My love…"

"There's no time! Marianne, run! Hide!" Desmonda said tugging Sage back to face her. "Sage, you must help us give her time to escape. Help us hold the demon in the circle."

Marianne took several backward steps, watching as Sage nodded. Desmonda pulled him away.

"Go, Marianne!" With one last look, he turned to confront the demon with the two spellcasters at his side. Sage lifted his hands, a ball of flame extending from his fingertips, then blasted into the circle to keep the demon locked away from Marianne.

Marianne's legs bumped against a gravestone, shivering as the stone passed through her. Then she turned and ran into the darkness.

****

Sage kept slinging fireballs at the circle, to keep the demon distracted while Marianne escaped behind him. After a while, he realized his magic was having little to no effect on the demon. The only one seemingly able to control the circle was Michael, and just barely. The man was nearly to his knees. Sweat drenched his hair and stained his collar. He held his arms high, the power flowing from his fingertips even as the demon surged against him.

"Enough," Sage said, lowering his arms. Chills shivered along his skin when the demon's gaze met his. "Leave Marianne alone. I'll come with you. Willingly."

"Sage, you don't know what you're doing!" Desmonda's voice echoed eerily behind him.

The flames surrounding the circle died down until Sage could meet the demon face to face with nothing between them.

"I've a taste for a body of my own. When I answered Drake's summons, he forbid me from taking your ginger-haired beauty. Seeing as how he no longer has possession of her body, I'm no longer obligated to obey his commands."

"Leave her be. Take me instead!"

The demon shook her head. "Our time together was precious, but I need you no longer."

A flash of smoke and fire filled the space, swallowing the demon. When the circle cleared, the demon was nowhere to be seen.

"I've lost it," Michael said, falling to his knees. Desmonda rushed to his side.

But Sage turned away, looking beyond the graveyard behind them into the dark forest where Marianne had vanished.

"Marianne," he whispered. Pain swelled in his heart at the thought of Marianne falling into the demon's clutches. The memory of his own torment at the demon's hands haunted him. What damage would the creature do to an innocent such as Marianne?

How could he stop it? How could he protect Marianne? He didn't have the correct spells or the magic. Even a sorcerer had difficulty controlling the demon.

Sage glanced back to where Desmonda comforted Michael. The reverend lay prone on the ground. The half-demon bent over him, running her fingers through his hair and along one cheek. Then she placed her lips on his.

The sight shocked him.

Were they lovers? The way they stared into each other's eyes, it seemed only those truly in love would hold and kiss each other with such tenderness. Sage hadn't seen the connection before, perhaps because he was so focused on freeing himself from the demon's curse. But it was obvious Michael was beloved in Desmonda's eyes.

Beloved.

The word crept into his mind, weaving through the possibilities. And then as if someone suddenly cast a light spell that brightened a dark room, he knew.

Only a beloved could break the spell cast over Marianne.

"I know what to do to save Marianne."

****

Marianne ran for hours through the dark forest. If she had been corporeal, she would have stumbled through the brush, injuring herself and announcing her presence for miles around. As it was, she glided soundlessly along the forest floor, a ghost among the trees.

She stopped when the forest faded away to reveal a field. Beyond the farmer's field, the tall spires of another church rising into the moonlit sky.

Holy ground. Sanctuary. Surely, the demon could not find her there.

She hurried into the church, passing through the closed doors with nothing but a tingle of awareness to mark the solid object. Though the interior was dark, she saw enough shapes illuminated from the moon's light cast through the windows to find a pew and sink into it.

If she'd been human, she'd be struggling for breath

from the frantic running. But her heart hammered in fright rather than exhaustion. She reckoned she could keep running indefinitely seeing as she was a spirit.

Why hadn't she thought of finding safety in the confines of that other church where she and Sage had met Miss Green? It would have saved her being parted from Sage.

Now that she felt safe again, her thoughts returned to him. Was he still in danger? Had Michael freed Sage from the demon's curse?

Questions plagued her as she sat in the still darkness, waiting. Waiting for what? How long must she sit? Sage would never know where to find her. But if Marianne set foot outside the church, she'd become vulnerable. The demon might catch her.

Marianne shuddered.

She wondered if Sage was safe. She wanted to go back, to search the area for him, but it was too dangerous.

For her and Sage.

Better to sit and wait.

Marianne groaned. She dropped her head onto her arms resting on the pew in front of her.

Perhaps it was better to find Sage. To fight. Instead of hiding and waiting.

A rustling noise echoed in the darkness. She lifted her head. Was it Sage? Had he followed her?

A shadow moved at the back of the church. She opened her mouth to call out to him, thinking it must be Sage, but hesitated.

What if it wasn't Sage?

Although if it were not Sage, what difference would it make if she called out or not? Only three people could see or hear her so she'd be in no danger unless it was the demon. And everyone knew demons could not cross onto holy ground. She was safe enough as long as she stayed on church grounds.

"Hello?" Marianne called out. If it were Sage come to search for her and she remained silent, he might miss her in the darkness and move on in his search.

The shadow stopped, then changed direction toward Marianne. Expecting him to say something, she waited. As he stepped closer, she realized of the shape this person's body did not match Sage.

She stood.

The shadow approached, and Marianne could identify the silhouette of a woman. When she walked into a pool of moonlight, Marianne looked into her glowing red eyes.

"Hello, Marianne."

She screamed.

Chapter Fifteen

"Has he arrived?" Sage asked as he leapt from the carriage, rushing toward the entrance of Merriweather Manor.

Basil stood at the door to greet him.

"He's in the parlor."

"Good."

"Care to explain your plan?"

"No need," Sage said, quickly. "I'll show you." He strode passed his bewildered brother, vaguely aware Basil followed close behind as he made his way to the parlor. Sage opened the door, frightening Julia who sat closest. She jumped as he charged in.

"Julia, how do you do?" He nodded in her direction, but paid her no mind after his brief greeting. Instead, he scanned the room like a hunter searching for prey. His eyes narrowed on David Fernsby who sat next to Julia at the table in the corner of the room, sipping tea. At Sage's bold entrance, Fernsby let out a squeal, his eyes as wide as the saucer that currently trembled in his hand, the cup quaking in midair as he stared at the intruder.

"You," Sage said, pointing with a scowl at the young man.

"Me?"

"Yes. Come with me."

"Sage? What's this all about?" He heard Julia's

inquiries, but he did not pause to answer. Instead, he backed away, waiting rather impatiently for Fernsby to gather the courage necessary to stand and follow. It took a moment, but with a glowering look from Sage, Fernsby leapt to his feet and hurried after. Sage led Fernsby, as well as the others who trailed after, up the stairs and through the halls until he found Marianne's bedchamber.

He hesitated outside the room for a moment, staring at the grains of wood on the door and taking several deep breaths. It was just as well he hesitated. Basil and Fernsby were still hurrying to catch him up, Julia waddling close behind in her advanced state of pregnancy.

But Sage hesitated for a reason other than allowing the others to follow him. A reason he was ashamed to admit. As much as he wanted Marianne's curse to be lifted, he was loathe to admit he needed Fernsby's help.

Mrs. Watson's admission still rang loudly in his ears. To her knowledge, young Fernsby was quite smitten with Marianne. The young cad loved her.

And Sage loathed him for it.

Fernsby did not deserve Marianne. Her goodness and light were too much for a boy like him to appreciate.

Mrs. Watson had heard of the rumors Miss Smythe had spread, of Fernsby's intentions of asking for her hand. None of it was true. Charlotte was mistaken. Fernsby had no plans to marry anyone save Marianne.

There was a demon to consider, however, which compelled Sage to turn the handle and open the door, hurrying Fernsby to follow.

"Marianne?" Fernsby said, stopping at the

entrance.

"Come along, young Fernsby, we have no time to delay." Sage reached for the man's arm, dragging him with him as he approached the bed with the body of Marianne poised upon the sheets.

"This is quite unorthodox," Fernsby mumbled.

Basil hurried to his brother's side. "Do you know what you're doing?" he whispered in Sage's ear.

"Yes," Sage answered with a nod. "I'm saving Marianne."

From the corner of his eye, Sage saw Julia in the doorway, slightly out of breath from the chase through the halls. Basil moved to take her hand. His brother's blond head leaned toward her to whisper in her ear.

"Now, Fernsby," Sage began, wondering yet again how he was going to pull this off. "Do us a favor, will you? Kiss Miss Marianne." He gestured to the figure on the bed.

Fernsby, who stood several inches shorter than Sage's towering height, leaned up and whispered, "She's sleeping."

"Yes."

"I don't wish to wake her."

"It's imperative you wake her."

"That's quite rude, is it not?"

"Not in this case," Sage said. Taking Fernsby by the shoulders, he positioned him next to the bed. "We're in a bit of a bind, Fernsby. Let us say we're having difficulty waking the charming Miss Marianne. I think she'd be quite pleased for you to kiss her until she woke."

"Please do," Julia said softly from the doorway. Fernsby glanced in her direction, his eyes widening at the sight of her pale, drawn face.

"What's this all about?" Wariness crept into his voice. Sage felt the man stiffen beneath the pressure of his fingers holding him in place.

"It's too much to go on about now. How's about I pay you twenty shillings to kiss the girl? Will that do?" Basil asked, reaching into his pockets to produce the coin.

"See, here," Fernsby said, bristling. "I'm not about to take bribes to kiss an innocent girl—"

"Fifty pounds," Sage said.

"Done." Fernsby shrugged away from Sage's grip, sinking onto the bed beside Marianne. He placed one hand on her shoulder, the other on the mattress and leaned down to place his lips solidly on hers. It was the most chaste of kisses, brief and brotherly. When Fernsby pulled away Sage bent over her, wanting to be the first to see Marianne's eyes open.

He waited.

Nothing happened.

"Do it again."

"What?"

"Kiss her again," Sage snapped, his gaze never leaving Marianne's face. His heart thumped painfully in his chest. The air in the room felt thick and heavy, so much so he had difficulty breathing. But he focused on her face, waiting for any flicker of movement, any sign of her spirit returning to her body.

Fernsby bent down and kissed her again. The sound of his lips smacking on hers echoed in the silent room.

"Marianne?" Fernsby leaned back to peer closely at her face. "Marianne, are you awake? Is this some sort of jest?" When she remained unresponsive, he glanced back at Sage and Basil. "What's going on here? Is there something wrong with her?"

Basil stepped forward, taking Fernsby by the arm and lifting him from the bed.

"Perhaps you might come with us," Basil said, dragging him to the door.

"No," Sage protested, his hand darting out to take Fernsby's other arm, keeping him trapped between them. "I need him."

"It's not working, Sage."

"It must work. There's no other way."

"Sage—"

But he was finished listening. He grabbed Fernsby by the lapels of his jacket.

"Do you love Marianne?"

"What?"

"Answer me! Do you love her?"

"Well, of course, that is…I mean…I care a great deal for her…"

"Do you love her?" Sage repeated the question, but his grip on Fernsby had slackened as the man attempted to answer him. It was a simple answer of yes or no. Why couldn't he say it?

"I'm intensely *fond* of the girl, to be sure."

Oh, God.

Harriet Watson was mistaken. David Fernsby did not love Marianne. Not with the passion of a beloved who might possess the strength of love to break the spell cast over her.

Sage released the man and stepped back from him. His hands fell to his sides, clenching with the strong desire to smash the in young fop's face.

"Julia," Basil said, coming to stand between Sage and Marianne's would-be beloved. "Would you be so kind as to accompany Mr. Fernsby to the parlor? I believe Cook has prepared some cucumber sandwiches. I'll remain here to have a word with my brother. Mr. Fernsby, I promise you an explanation the moment I arrive. Have patience with us, I beg of you."

Sage allowed Basil to take the mumbling Fernsby away. The young man followed Julia out of the room. As soon as the door clicked shut, Sage's gaze returned to his brother.

"This was a foolish notion, Sage. You've put us in a dangerous and awkward predicament. I'm not certain what I can say to convince this young man not to run back to London with all sorts of mad tales about the Merriweathers paying for men to kiss the comatose Miss Grey."

"Paying was your idea."

"Be that as it may," Basil said, raising his hand to stop any more of Sage's rebuttal. "I think we should have discussed this before leaping—"

"A demon is after Marianne," Sage said, silencing his brother. "The same demon that attacked us at Castle Blackmoor."

"What?"

"Miss Green and her associate summoned the demon with plans to break the bond it placed on me. Something went wrong. The demon promised to release me in exchange for Marianne. If it gets her spirit, it can possess her body completely. We'll lose Marianne forever."

"Gods and goddesses above," Basil muttered, backing up to sink into a chair next to the bed.

"Miss Green assisted us with finding a way to break the spell cast over Marianne. It's an ancient spell. Marianne needs the token of her beloved to wake her. I realized the token must be a kiss of the man who loves her most. I mistakenly believed it to be Fernsby." Sage gestured at the door, then turned to sit onto the mattress beside Marianne. He lifted her hand, cradling, stroking her slender fingers in his.

"She loves him," he continued. He felt the pinch of tears gathering in the corners of his eyes. "She speaks of him often."

Basil didn't say anything. There were no words after all. Nothing that could help her now.

He'd failed her.

The tears fell then, drops splashing onto the smooth skin of Marianne's warm hand.

"Where is she now?"

"Hiding. Desmonda told her to run. It will do no good. The demon will find her. We'll know when it does. Marianne will wake, but it won't be her."

"You must kill her," a voice said. Sage's head lifted to discover Desmonda Green standing in the open doorway. He hadn't heard her enter.

Julia's bewildered face hovered behind her shoulder. "What did you say?"

Desmonda looked at neither Basil nor Julia, but focused on Sage. "If she wakes and the demon possesses her, you must kill her."

"Never," Sage growled.

"You must. There's nowhere for Marianne's spirit to hide that the demon will not find her. Once the demon takes possession of her spirit, it will slip into her body giving it access to this world without the control of a summoner. It will wreak havoc. Destruction. It must be stopped before it can destroy us."

"No. I will not kill Marianne!"

"No!" Julia's cry caught Basil's attention. He rushed to his wife.

Desmonda advanced into the room, her hand vanishing into the folds of her skirts. When it reappeared, it held a dagger.

"If you cannot, then I will do it."

"Do not!" Sage stood, placing himself between Marianne's body and the approaching half-demon.

"You understand. It will no longer *be* Marianne. Her soul will never return to her body. The demon won't allow it. Even now it might have possession of her."

"You don't know that."

"Either way, *when* it happens, we must destroy the demon. You, of all people, know what damage a demon can do. Would you have the rest of your family surrender to the demon's will? Would you allow it access to your brother, his wife, his unborn child?"

"No!" Sage roared. The thought of the cursed demon anywhere near his brother's family sent uncontrollable rage coursing through him. His chest constricted. The room seemed to dim as his vision narrowed onto Desmonda Green. His fingers burned, but he suppressed the flame that threatened to emerge.

"No one can help Marianne, now. If the beloved's token did not work to break the spell, nothing will. David Fernsby was the last man who could save her. You know what I say is true."

Sage closed the gap between them, wrapping his hands around her wrists, trapping her, stopping her, keeping the deadly sharp dagger from reaching Marianne.

"No! She's my sister! You can't!" Julia's screams echoed from the hall where Basil dragged his crying wife from the room.

"You will not touch her." Sage peeled the dagger from Desmonda's fingers.

"You must kill her," she repeated, staring into his eyes, willing him to understand.

He did.

Only too well.

He couldn't allow the demon to possess Marianne. But he couldn't give up on her yet. Could he?

Indecision wracked his brain.

He lifted his hands, clasping them against his head as he let out a roar of internal pain so fierce it felt physical. His heart was breaking, shattering, smashing into infinitesimal pieces that he knew he'd have no hope of ever putting back together.

"Sage…" Desmonda said.

"Enough!" He shouted. He rubbed his free hand against his eyes, swiping at the tears that blinded him. "Go."

"You must—"

"Go…before I use this dagger on you, as well." His warning felt like a confession. Desmonda backed away, breathing a sigh of relief as she understood what he meant to do. Julia screamed as if Sage thrust the dagger into her body instead of her sister's. Basil dragged his wife away, her screams fading. But it was Sage's heart that felt the blade. The weapon weighed heavily in his hand. His fingers clenched the handle, thoughts of what he must do sickened him. Grief coiled around his soul.

After tonight, he'd never be the same again.

How could he live without Marianne? Without her endless chatter, her constant company, her wicked wit and vibrant laughter? He didn't know a life without Marianne. She'd always been with him. From the time she was born, she'd been part of his life, his heart. Even before he realized how his feelings had changed for her, how much he'd come to love her, she'd always touched a part of him.

He didn't want to know a life without Marianne.

Thoughts of ending his pain caressed the edge of his consciousness. Hadn't he been through enough grief? His parents' death when he was young, the discovery of Basil's terminal condition, Drake's wife's death leading to his brother's descent into madness, the demon's attack and torture and now...ending the life of a woman who meant more than the world to him.

.Did he not bear the burden of enough pain? And the question remained...how could Sage go on living with Marianne's blood on his hands? She trusted him. She looked to him to protect her, save her. Instead, he would bring her death.

How quick could the dagger go from Marianne's body to his?

That new question lingered, teasing his thoughts as his soul felt the crush of agony.

He sank onto the mattress beside her, reaching out to cup her cheek with his free hand, the dagger poised on his lap. Her skin felt silky smooth and warm.

She was so beautiful. The most beautiful creature he'd ever seen. No one had ever compared to her. He realized how blind he had been for these many years, not to acknowledge the beauty in front of him all of this time.

He wept. It didn't matter if the half-demon watched silently from across the room, or if his brother battled with Julia somewhere in the hall. Sage let the tears fall for his beautiful Marianne. The woman he could not save.

Sage bent over her, resting his forehead against hers, inhaling her scent, her breath. He closed his eyes and let the feel of her press against his skin. This was all he had of her. An empty shell.

Where was she now? Alone, running for her life. A life she had yet to know was at an end. Was she frightened? Did she await his rescue?

He trembled.

"Marianne," he whispered against her skin. "Come back to me, my love." He rained kisses across her forehead, down her cheeks as he raised the dagger up between them, placing the sharpened edge along the length of pale cream of her neck. A quick thrust and it would be done, and then he could finish himself.

"Meet me in the ever-after, my darling, and we will walk among the world of our ancestors. Together. Hand in hand. Please, Marianne…"

He kissed the lids of her eyes, the tip of her nose.

"I love you, my heart."

One last kiss before he ended it. He placed his lips over hers, pressing the dagger close. This was how he'd finish it. A kiss, with their blood mingling. With any luck, their deaths would be quick, and their bond would be strong enough to find each other in the ever-after.

And then her lips opened.

Her body moved beneath him, and she was kissing him back. It was a dream, he knew. Perhaps he had thrust the dagger and was dead already. He deepened the kiss, pulling her breath into him, her very being so she became a part of him.

Her arms came up, holding him against her. And then she broke away from the kiss to say his name.

"Sage."

The sound of her soft murmur thrilled him. Warmth spread throughout his body, hardening him. His desire for her was unquestionable. All the lost moments he'd had in the past, all those times he might have wooed her, charmed her, loved her. He had let them all slip away.

Now too late, he had the opportunity to show her how he felt for her.

He let the forgotten dagger slip from between them. Easily he dropped it to the floor, not daring to see their blood staining the blade.

With both hands free, he gathered her into his arms, wrapping himself around her to hold her, keep her close. He'd never let her go again.

"Is this real?" Her breath was a gentle wind against his cheek.

"No." He shook his head, his skin brushing against hers. "It no longer matters. Nothing matters, but you're here with me, at last."

He kissed her again, this time with more desperation. He ravaged her mouth, softening only when he heard her whimpers. Having no wish to hurt her, he began to draw away, but her hands gripped his shoulders, keeping him in place.

Being this was either dream or death, it seemed just that she would welcome him. In life Marianne would never have slipped her legs around his to tangle her limbs against him. She would never have whispered his name with such wanton desire. Nor would she have looked at him with those dreamy eyes as if he was the shining knight as told in so many stories come to her rescue.

Tears crept back into his eyes.

"What's this?" Her fingertips brushed against the wetness that had fallen onto her cheek.

"I'm sorry, Marianne. I'm so sorry I couldn't save you. I failed you."

"Shh…" She moved a finger to his lips. "I'm here now."

He nodded. Then lowered his head to her neck where he kissed and nibbled the skin. Her gasp of delight encouraged him to reach further. He traveled to the bodice of her gown, slipping his fingers beneath the fabric to gently enfold one silky breast in his hand. The peak stiffened at his touch, and he bent to take one tip in his mouth.

She gasped.

His blood thrummed through his body, his heart beat a fierce rhythm, singing a song of love for Marianne. This was his moment. His chance to shower affection upon her. To show without words how his heart was hers alone.

He touched her body, feeling her heat through the thin fabric of her gown. She opened her legs, and he touched the juncture of her thighs. Her back arched; a little whimper escaped her lips. When he looked up, her face turned to one side, her eyes closed, her hands reaching into her hair to grasp the strawberry locks.

With one hand, he bunched the fabric of her dress, gathering it upward until her body lay exposed. She wore nothing beneath.

The sight of her nude body thrilled him, spurring him on like an untried youth. He craved her, knew he couldn't wait; he must have her.

He unfastened his breeches, his hardness springing forth in eagerness.

Before he could go any further, her hand was there, tentatively touching him, caressing him, squeezing him.

He closed his eyes and groaned.

"Did I hurt you?"

"Quite the opposite. You give me incredible pleasure."

She continued to stroke him. He marveled at the capacity of love he felt for her. He never thought to feel such a way about another human being. To care so deeply, so passionately, that the rest of the world fell away completely. It was only the two of them, in this moment, and he hoped this was the Heaven they spoke of during those Sunday church outings he had been forced to attend as a child so they could better blend in with the community. If this is what welcomed him after death, he would never regret the decisions he had made.

"Sage." She whispered his name on a soft moan escaping her lips.

He pulled her hand away to position himself at her opening. Then he pushed into her. Her slick heat welcomed him, and he felt at last he had found where he belonged. This was his home, his heart, his world. He was one half of a whole with this woman completing his soul.

Marianne's hands were undoing the buttons of his shirt until she could slip her fingers across the skin of his chest. She writhed beneath him, her hips moving to welcome each thrust. Her eagerness warmed him, thrilled him, made him want to show her more, show her everything they could attain together, take her to the summit where he could show her how to reach the stars with him.

But to his dismay, he could not wait for this time. In his excitement, his lust for her overwhelmed him and he was spilling his seed into her. Then she was with him, calling his name, her muscles squeezing around him, her body clenching as those beautiful spasms shivered across her skin. They fell back to the world together, clutching each other.

He held her to him, closing his eyes as he rested his head next to hers.

"I love you, Marianne," he whispered. "I love you. I love you."

"This is amazing. What a beautiful dream," Marianne whispered back, her fingers caressing the flesh on his chest. "I wish all my dreams were as wonderful as this."

He smiled, filled with contentment. So much that he didn't respond to the sound of the door opening. He was dead, so what did he care for doors?

"Ah, here you are. I simply *knew* this is where I'd find you."

A sick chill vibrated through Sage's body at the sultry tones of the woman who walked into the room. He looked up. The demon walked slowly toward them.

He grabbed Marianne's shoulders and dragged her with him as he slid off the bed. Quickly, he fastened his trousers as he faced the demon. From the corner of his vision, he saw Marianne cover her bare breasts with her bodice.

What was this? They were dead. How could the demon find them beyond death?

"I was that close," she said, holding up her hands to show a small space between. "I found her in a church. *A church*! She thought to hide from me there. As if the power of any god might save her. Foolish child." The demon glanced at Marianne, smirking. "But just as I was about to take her for my own, she vanished. What magic is this, I wondered? Who had the power to help her escape? And then I knew…"

Her red gaze leveled onto his. The power of her evil sent a shiver of fear along his spine. He raised his hands to prepare his defensive magic, knowing it wouldn't work. He had no magic to save them.

His heart continued to thunder as he stared at the approaching creature. The reality of the situation hit him.

He wasn't dead.

Nor was Marianne.

The curse was lifted.

He'd broken the spell cast over her. *He* did it. Not Fernsby. That could only mean one thing…

He was Marianne's beloved.

At a moment when he should have felt such joy, fear coursed through his veins as the demon approached.

She crept closer, her attention narrowing on Sage.

"You've been practicing new magic. I can smell it on you. Since you've taken my prize from me, my dear sweet Sage, I suppose I'll take you back with me instead. I did so enjoy our time together."

She grinned and attacked.

Chapter Sixteen

It wasn't a dream!

Marianne had no time to discover just how her spirit managed to get pulled back into her corporeal form. The demon advanced on Sage, its face twisting in rage.

Marianne took a stance beside him, ready to assist with whatever magic ability she possessed.

"Get back, Marianne," Sage ordered when he noticed her step forward.

"I can help." She hoped. Swallowing hard passed the lump in her throat, she wondered if she had *any* magic ability left. She wouldn't know until she cast if there were any lasting effects from the spell. It had nearly been a year, after all, since she had cast a proper spell. Would the time spent outside her body have done any damage?

"Fool," the demon growled. "You cannot stop me!"

It threw its power against them. Sage blocked it, then cast a spell against it. As before, his magic turned to flame. The fire poured onto the demon.

She laughed. "That tickles."

Marianne took a moment to cast an attack spell, pushing it forward into the demon's chest with all of her might. The demon barely noticed. Instead of falling back as Marianne had hoped, it turned to her instead. The demon's image shimmered, and suddenly she was looking at her father.

"My pet," he said. "Why would you hurt me?"

"Papa?"

"She's a chameleon, Marianne. That's not your father," Sage said, as he cast another spell. Marianne watched her father flinch as the fire from Sage's spell burned him. He fell back, his hands raised to protect his face. He screamed.

Terror squeezed Marianne's chest. She reacted instinctively, stepping forward to protect him. Was it her father? Perhaps the demon held him captive? Perhaps he wasn't dead?

"No, Marianne," Sage said, pulling her back before she could walk into the flame's path. "It can take the form of any it chooses. Marianne, look at its eyes. It's not your father."

That's when she recognized the red glow coming from her father's eyes. She hadn't seen it before. The demon must have masked it in some way.

She whimpered in renewed grief. That barely held hope her father yet lived was crushed.

The demon, still molded in her father's image, straightened and laughed. "If I had been thinking, I should have come to you in the church as this. Yes, this would have done nicely." And the demon's image shifted again. This time, it was Sage looking at her. A perfect replica…the same dark hair, body, face. Everything. Except for the eyes. They glowed red. "Since your spirit is now reunited with your body, I cannot claim you. But I'll have my Sage. Yes, Sage and I will have fun together."

"No," Marianne said, then raised her hands to prepare another attack spell. "I love him! With all my heart I love him, and you will never touch him again!" She flung the spell. Surprisingly, the impact sent the demon back a step.

Sage looked at Marianne. "You love me?"

"Yes, you twit!" Marianne shouted, focusing on the demon as it shrugged off the spell and advanced.

Sage stepped in front of her, shielding her. Then he swung at the copy of himself, landing a solid punch to the jaw. The demon repeated Sage's move, only when it connected with Sage's jaw, Sage was flung into the air. He hit the wall hard, his head smashing into a portrait hung there. When he slid to the floor, he slumped forward and did not move.

Marianne gasped.

Was he dead?

The urge to run to his side compelled her to take a step forward, but the demon stepped between them.

Marianne's foot bumped against a forgotten object on the floor. She stooped to pick it up. It was the dagger Sage had been holding when she awoke on the bed. The question of what he was doing with it tickled her consciousness, but she pushed it aside. Now was not the time.

"And what do you think to do with that?" the demon asked, Sage's face smiling with derision back at her.

Marianne didn't speak. She flung the dagger into the demon's face. It struck one fiery eye, embedding the blade deep into the flesh. The demon fell back, screaming. Its image flickered, and again it was the woman with dark hair.

Marianne ran to where Sage lay on the floor, kneeling beside him to check if his chest rose and fell.

It did. Then she looked back to watch the demon pull the protruding dagger from its face. Blood gushed from the wound, thick and black.

The door opened at the same moment.

Both Marianne and the demon turned to face the new intruder.

Miss Prescott entered, her snow-white hair bundled in tiny curls atop her head. She held a cane in one hand, using it to assist her to step into the room since her one knee was crotchety. The elderly woman took in the scene, her mouth pursing into a thin line of disapproval.

A man followed behind her. Marianne did not recognize him, but she thought his blue eyes looked oddly familiar. He was dressed elegantly, his clothes revealing his wealth. With his back rigid, he held the air of a gentleman.

"Who has been summoning demons in my house?" Miss Prescott glanced at Sage's slumped form on the floor. "Ah, yes, I should have suspected. Oh, Marianne. Good to see you finally awake, child."

"Aunt Petunia?" Sage mumbled as he blinked, then struggled to sit up. Marianne assisted him, propping him against the wall. "You! What are you doing here?" Sage struggled to stand when he saw the man enter the room behind his aunt.

The man held his hands before him in a gesture of peace. "I mean no harm. Hello, Miss Marianne. Good to see you once more." The gentleman smiled.

Marianne gasped as she recognized him. He was one of the highwaymen! The one with the powder.

"I thought you had more sense than this, Sage. Messing with demons. What were you thinking?"

"Aunt Petunia, run. You must…"

The demon turned to the elderly witch and growled.

Miss Prescott's eyes narrowed.

The highwayman stepped around the elderly woman, pulling a pistol from inside his jacket.

"Miss Prescott, at your convenience."

"Jack, you must be daft!" Miss Prescott pushed her way around the highwayman to face the demon. "Oh, begone with you and never return!" She raised her cane, waving it in the air as a wand, spoke a few words and smoke billowed around the demon. The creature growled and howled as the smoke rose like a blanket around it. Slowly the blanket grew smaller until there nothing but a wisp floating in the air. In the end, even that disappeared along with the demon's growls.

There was a sucking noise and a pop, then silence.

"Melodramatic beasts," Miss Prescott muttered, returning her cane to her side.

"What did you…? How?" Sage stammered.

"I'll be honest. I was not certain that would work." Jack, the highwayman, lowered his pistol. The stunned expression on his face might have been amusing another time.

"I sensed the creature the moment it manifested on the grounds outside. I've cast a protective spell around Merriweather Manor, something to keep such nasties from our door. Sage, I'm disappointed in you, my boy. I thought you knew never to deal with demons."

"Auntie, I…"

"Never you mind," she interrupted. "Basil has already informed me of your predicament, and Mr. John Winters here has filled me in with some other details that I find rather shocking. Really," she said, pausing to tap her cane on the floor. "The trouble you boys get yourselves into...It's disgraceful. And instead of coming to your elders for assistance and advice, you rough it out and deal with it yourselves. Well, I should let you suffer this curse to teach you a lesson, but seeing as I don't want any more demons sniffing around..."

Again she lifted the cane as a wand, raised her other hand and summoned power. A few quick words Marianne could not decipher and a light appeared from the tip of the wand.

The light was dim at first, but it grew brighter as Miss Prescott closed her eyes and whispered. Then she flung the light at Sage. He stiffened when the beam hit him; his eyes widened and his fingers clenched. A moment later, he collapsed.

"Sage!"

"He'll be fine in a moment, my dear. His body must rid itself of the black magic that has sickened it. Demon's curses..." Miss Prescott's gaze softened as she looked down at him. "My poor boy...How he must have suffered."

Marianne nodded. She held his hand while he slept, wishing she could make him more comfortable on the floor.

Miss Prescott waved her cane. The chair that sat across the room slid silently across the carpet. When it arrived at Sage's side, Miss Prescott sat down.

"What did you do with the demon? Did you kill it?" Marianne asked.

"No, my dear. It's quite difficult to kill a demon. This one did not have a human body to hold it permanently to our world, so I sent it back to its dark domain. But, it will never again return to Merriweather Manor. I will see to that."

"How did you know what to do?"

"Jack." Miss Prescott waved her cane at the highwayman standing next to her. "Mr. Winters arrived hours ago with a message from Drake. Jack has been helping me practice the spell to lift the curse placed on Sage. And he assisted with the protective spell we cast around Merriweather Manor. It should protect us from the more nasty creatures in this world."

"Do you know who summoned the demon?"

The old woman's lips pursed again. She nodded. "I do. And we must deal with him soon enough."

"And do you know what this man tried to do to us on the road?" Marianne nodded toward the highwayman.

"My apologies, Miss Marianne." Jack Winters stepped forward. "I'm an associate of Drake Merriweather's. He sent me to administer that powder. He suspected it might break the curse cast upon you."

"He means to make amends then?"

Mr. Winters shook his head. "Still experimenting, I'm afraid. Seeing as it was supposed to do you good, I saw no reason to deny him. I see it did indeed cure you."

"Not quite," Marianne admitted. "Sage was all I needed."

Miss Petunia sighed. "The madness has consumed Drake. Something must be done. At least he was sensible enough to send round Jack when he lost control of the demon. Apparently it informed him of his intentions with Sage. There's hope for our Drake, I'm certain of it."

Marianne might have disagreed, but Sage moaned, and his eyelids flickered. Soon he was sitting up, looking astonished at his aunt and Marianne who smiled down upon him.

"What happened?"

"You explain, my dear," Miss Prescott announced, tapping her cane on the floor and moving to stand. "I believe I'll have Charles bring some tea to the parlor. You may join me, at your convenience, of course. Come along, Jack. You can finish telling me the tale about your brother." She smiled and quit the room, Mr. Winters at her heels.

Sage blinked, then turned his confused stare to Marianne. The moment their gazes locked, relief flooded his face and he smiled.

"Marianne."

She flung her arms around him, laughing with joy, relief and love. He held her, and she could feel the deep rumbles of laughter blossoming in his chest.

"My Marianne," he said, pulling her head away from his chest to hold her face in his hands. He caressed her cheek with his thumb.

"How did you do it?" Marianne asked. "What spell did you use to wake me?"

"Love," Sage answered. "Marianne, I love you. As more than a friend or brother or neighbor. I love you with my soul. I'd do anything to be with you forever."

"Oh, Sage…"

"I want you to promise me something, Marianne. Promise you'll never leave me again. Promise you'll be my wife. Promise we'll spend the rest of our days together, good and bad. I cannot bear to be parted from you."

Marianne smiled, tears of happiness sparkling her eyes. "I promise."

And he kissed her.

A word about the author...

Tricia Schneider is a paranormal and gothic romance author. Before the supernatural took possession of her pen, she worked for several years in a bookstore as assistant manager and bookseller. Now she writes full-time while raising her three young children. She lives with her musician husband and two neurotic cats in the coal country of Pennsylvania.

Learn more about her books at her website:
http://www.triciaschneider.com.

Thank you for purchasing
this publication of The Wild Rose Press, Inc.

If you enjoyed the story, we would appreciate your
letting others know by leaving a review.

For other wonderful stories,
please visit our on-line bookstore at
www.thewildrosepress.com.

For questions or more information
contact us at
info@thewildrosepress.com.

The Wild Rose Press, Inc.
www.thewildrosepress.com

Stay current with The Wild Rose Press, Inc.

Like us on Facebook

https://www.facebook.com/TheWildRosePress

And Follow us on Twitter
https://twitter.com/WildRosePress